day the

THE SCHEME

It was an exciting idea. It tantalized his imagination. All he had to do was apply the RS Theory of Teacher Handling to Silent Henry, and get Henry to tell him where the ginseng grows. It was the third week in September now, so that would mean about two weeks, maybe less, until the ginseng was ripe enough to dig. Then there would be at least two or three weekends before the season was over, and if he knew where to look for the ginseng, he should be able to harvest at least a thousand dollars' worth during those weekends.

The pleasant pain of excitement rose inside him. The idea wasn't a sure thing, but it was more fun that way, more of a challenge. The RS Theory had certainly worked on his teachers. He could think of no reason why it wouldn't work equally well on Henry, and with Henry the stakes were worth the struggle. He would be playing the game, not for better grades with less work, but for money.

Lots of money.

Lynn Hall

The Siege of Silent Henry

AVON
PUBLISHERS OF BARD, CAMELOT AND DISCUS BOOKS

AVON BOOKS
A division of
The Hearst Corporation
959 Eighth Avenue
New York, New York 10019

Copyright © 1972 by Lynn Hall
Published by arrangement with Follett Publishing Company.
Library of Congress Catalog Card Number: 72-2789
ISBN: 0-380-01744-X

First Avon Printing, August, 1977

AVON TRADEMARK REG. U.S. PAT. OFF. AND IN
OTHER COUNTRIES, MARCA REGISTRADA,
HECHO EN U.S.A.

Printed in the U.S.A.

1

All of his best ideas came to him slowly. They were formed in the basement of his mind, when random bits of information were drawn together by his imagination and shaped by the mixture of knowledge and needs that was, uniquely, Robert Short.

During this forming time, before the idea rose to the brightly lit upstairs of his conscious mind, Robert felt restless, almost depressed. Unexplainable tensions kept him stirring in his seat at school or pacing from room to room at home.

Today had been that kind of day, but at first he didn't recognize the symptoms. The blue-and-gold September afternoon, wasting itself beyond the hermetically sealed windows of the high school building, would have been reason enough for his unsettled mood, and so would the fact that RS-15 was due to have her babies today.

But by the time the final bell had released him and the school bus had begun its five-mile run to Buck Creek, Robert knew an idea was about to come to him.

He sat alone, in the seat over the right rear wheel. Even though the school year was only three weeks old, seating arrangements were already firm—the young children up front where Mack could keep an eye on them; the older riders polarized into groups of twos and fours

5

according to ages, sex, and friendships. This particular seat, over the right rear wheel, belonged to Robert alone. No one else ever sat there. Robert enjoyed this quiet time between school and home. It was a good time to think, to make the transition from one world to the other.

He arranged his legs around the green metal wheel hump, and concentrated on holding his mind open for the idea.

I bet it'll be something about money, he thought, with the same anticipation he used to feel, looking at a Christmas package and thinking, I bet it's a chemistry set. In a way, this was even more exciting because the idea brewing in the back of his mind would be a toy of his own creation.

For the past few years, ever since he became aware that he had a mental agility his friends couldn't match, Robert's mind had been a source of pleasure to him, of unselfconscious delight. He thought of it as a miniature but perfect computer. Feed it random facts and it gives back conclusions, understanding, ideas. Feed it a seemingly insoluble problem, leave it alone for a few hours or a few days, and then, when the problem itself is all but forgotten, the computer offers up a solution. The RS Theory of Teacher Handling had come to him that way, and so had his Theory of Profitable Chinchilla Raising.

The problem with which he had been thinking himself to sleep all week was money, so he expected the idea now fighting its way to the surface would be an answer to this problem. But he knew from past experience that there was no way to force a new idea into the open until it was ready to come.

The bus stopped to let off Meredith Trost. As soon as it started up again, the girl who had been sitting with

Meredith rose and came swaying down the aisle toward Robert.

Amber was a thin-faced girl whose natural lack of sparkle seemed more noticeable when she came near Robert. The three of them, Amber, Meredith, and Robert, were the only high school students who still rode the Buck Creek school bus, most of the others having access to cars or friends with cars. As youngsters they had been close friends, finding and camouflaging secret caves in the bluffs, spying on Silent Henry to try to find the old man's wild ginseng beds, sharing their first pilfered pack of Lucky Strikes. But for the past few years complications had walled Robert away from the girls. Even in junior high he had stepped naturally into a higher social level than either of them. The strain of this difference made it impossible for the girls to relax in his presence. As for Robert, although he liked Amber well enough, he knew that when he got around to dating it would not be with her.

She stopped beside him and braced her hip against the seat back. "Did you get the English assignment?" Her voice had a rather forced quality, as though the sentence had been rehearsed.

He knew she was hoping he would remove his books from the empty seat beside him; he knew it wouldn't hurt him to let her ride the rest of the way with him and that it would probably mean a lot to her, but a core of stubbornness made him relish his power over her and withhold the invitation. He said, somewhat curtly, "Chapter Eight, read it and do the questions at the end."

"Chapter Eight?"

"Yeah."

"Oh. Well, thanks."

She swayed back up the aisle, leaving him with his

thoughts, but by then the idea that had seemed so near the surface was gone. He pressed his elbow against the narrow metal sill of the window and felt the vibrations of the highway all the way up his arm. By moving his elbow slowly across the ridge of the sill, he could come dangerously close to setting off the buzzing pain of the funny-bone nerve. He stopped just short of the point of pain.

The bus had turned east and was beginning the two-mile descent into Buck Creek. Close on either side of the highway rose densely wooded limestone slopes. Midway down, the narrow channel of the creek that gave the town its name joined the highway and followed close beside it on its winding way toward the river.

Just before the river came in sight, the valley widened slightly, and houses appeared. Most were old and tall and angular, built of cream-colored blocks of stone. The road came so close in front of them that it threatened their dignity, and the bluffs crowded in equally close from behind. On the creek-side of the road, footbridges of unpeeled logs or railroad ties spanned the creek bed in front of each house. From here on down, the lovely little spring-fed stream was known as "the ditch."

At the town's only corner the bus stopped and released Robert and Amber, along with a noisy scattering of younger children. Here, where the main street ended against a low flood dike, was the area loosely referred to as "downtown." Beyond the dike ran a single set of railroad tracks, a narrow green strip of park, and then the blue-and-gilt sweep of the Mississippi River.

A short block of stone buildings, originally warehouses and barrel-stave factories, looked out over the river with blank eyes. They stood as mute reminders that, a century and a half before, Buck Creek, Iowa, had been a booming market town and riverboat mecca. Now only the hotel was in use. It served as grocery store, tavern and cafe, town gathering place, and in the summer season, hotel.

Two elderly men sat in front of the hotel in folding canvas chairs. As Robert passed, they raised arthritic fingers in greeting, and nodded and smiled.

"Hi, Tom. Hi, Grampa."

"Robert," they muttered in unison. Grampa Severs was not related to Robert, but for many years he had been the town Grampa. By now even the middle-aged residents of Buck Creek had trouble remembering what Grampa's first name was. Four years ago, when Robert began insisting that people call him Robert instead of the detested Bobby, Grampa Severs had been the first to accept Robert's rule and to concede that a twelve-year-old had a right to choose his own name. Since then Robert had made a point of speaking to Grampa when he saw him, and he had felt mildly disloyal when he and his friends made fun of the old man behind his back.

Just south of the hotel the road curved past a row of large, ornately built frame houses that sat back against the foot of the bluff and looked out over the river. These houses had been built at the turn of the century by wealthy Chicagoans when, for that short period of time, Buck Creek had been a fashionable summer-home area.

Robert's house was one of these. It was blue and massive and neatly kept up, behind remnants of a wrought-iron fence. It had gingerbread trim, bay windows, and, on the inside, ornate filigree woodwork. He liked the house. He liked knowing that it was probably the best house in Buck Creek and that his mother decorated it with more taste than other Buck Creek housewives bothered to put into their homes.

The house was empty. He stood in the dining room and shouted, "Mom," but already the silence had told him she wasn't at home. Even when his mother was sitting perfectly still, which was almost never, her presence charged the house with an energy that was almost audible.

Robert went to the basement stairs and called, "I'll be right down." His answer was the softly metallic rustling of eighteen hungry chinchillas in their cages below him. It was an act of self-discipline that he put off checking on RS-15 until after he went upstairs and changed clothes.

The chinchillas were far more than a hobby for Robert. They were part of his life plan, which was, simply, to become a rich man. He had heard somewhere that no one becomes wealthy working for another man, and immediately he had decided that Robert Short was going to be his own boss. With this end in mind, he had set himself a goal of having ten-thousand dollars in the bank by the time his education was out of the way. In the past two years he had accumulated about fifteen hundred, plus enough to buy six of the best young chinchillas he could find.

When he had first begun looking into the possibility of chinchillas, he was struck by the fact that, a good pelt might sell for twenty-five dollars, but an equally good live animal, sold for breeding purposes, was worth ten times that much. Hence, the RS Theory of Profitable Chinchilla Raising: Start with animals good enough to win a few ribbons at chinchilla shows, and sell their offspring to other breeders who want to improve the quality of their stock. So far, it seemed to be working.

In jeans and tennis shoes, Robert bounced down the varnished open stairway, then down the narrower basement stairs and into the chinchilla room. The aluminum wire cages, built by him and his father, stood four tiers high against the back wall. Each cage housed a small blue-gray investment. They sat watching him like large-eared squirrels, their black eyes shining, their miniature front claws folded across bright white undersides. They were fat with fur and good breeding.

In one of the lower cages a large female whose ears bore the identifying tattoo "RS-15" huddled against her wire wall. Three mouse-sized miniatures of herself hopped near her. Although they were only a few hours old, their fur was fluffed and clean, and they moved with the agility of adult animals. Their eyes followed Robert's hand fearlessly as he picked them up one at a time for a closer look.

He handled them surely and gently. "Two females. Good old gal. You earned your raisin today." He moved slowly along the tiers of cages, slipping raisins through the wire into small snatching claws. Then, aware of the passing afternoon, he began to work more quickly, changing the newspapers under each tier of cages, refilling water bottles and pellet holders, and adding to his record book the births of RS-19, 20, and 21.

"Oh, you're home," his mother said as he emerged from the basement stairs. She had just come in the back door, with her arms around a Super-Value sack.

"No, I'm not home yet. I'm just a figment of your imagination."

"Good. Then you won't be looking for something to eat. Get away from those bananas. I need them for salad."

Miriam Short and her son might almost have passed for brother and sister at first glance. Her hair was soft

11

and dark, like his, and as yet showed no sign of gray. Robert was slight and wiry; his mother petite. She showed her approach to middle age only in a rounding out of face and hips. Still, she had about her a quality of childlike openness that age would never completely hide. It was from Miriam that Robert had inherited his fidgety energy.

He glanced up at the kitchen clock. A little after five. At least an hour till supper.

"I guess I'll walk out and meet Dad." He slammed out the back door before she could comment. He seldom walked anywhere, now that he was old enough to drive, and it was even more seldom that he walked out the mine road, or anyplace so deserted, for no more constructive reason than to ride home again with his father.

But the idea was stirring in his mind. He needed to be alone for a while to give it a chance.

Beyond Robert's house the blacktopped River Road narrowed and became the mine road. It gave up any pretense of paving for the rest of its mile or so of length. On the few occasions lately when Robert had walked the mine road, he told himself he should come out this way more often, but walking took time, and time was valuable to him.

The road closely followed the railroad track and the edge of the river, fifteen or twenty feet below. On his right, as Robert walked toward the mine, the land was dense with oak and birch trees whose limbs held mammoth ropes of grapevine. Behind the trees rose the towering limestone face of the bluffs.

A few of the trees already bore their fall coloring, and the bittersweet and sumac undergrowth was bright red and orange, but Robert's eyes saw only the dirt track ahead of his feet. His mind did not register the picture.

It sought to pick up the thread of his thoughts on the bus that afternoon, when he had felt so strongly that an idea was coming.

What have I been worrying about lately? he asked himself. What I'm going to do to earn some money this fall, I guess. Why can't this be Florida or someplace where I could work at the boat dock all winter? Seven-hundred dollars, free and clear, for working down there all summer. Not too bad, but it's still a long way from what I need. I won't have any chinchillas old enough to sell till after the first of the year. That's a lot of wasted time. September, October, November—what can I be doing . . .

At the crest of a small rise, Silent Henry Leffert's house came into view, below Robert on the river side of the road. A small thumb of land jutted into the river, leaving enough room between the riverbank and the railroad track for a house and a patch of lawn. The house had been built more than a hundred years ago as a brick factory, and was made of large soft-pink bricks, manufactured there. Although it was two stories high, it was just one room wide and deep, so that its dimensions reminded Robert of an upended orange crate. Its windows were half-circles, flat across the bottom, rounded on top.

Although it was an odd little house, it was so familiar to Robert that he seldom noticed it, and yet this afternoon the sight of Silent Henry's house caught Robert's attention and slowed his feet. He stared thoughtfully for a few minutes. Suddenly there was a shifting in his mind, and the idea was born.

2

Henry Leffert sucked in his breath as the pull of the
steering wheel angered the bursitis pain in his shoulder.
He got the old station wagon around the hotel corner
onto River Road, and relaxed somewhat. Just a short
stretch home, now. He raised his hand in greeting as he
passed Grampa Severs and Tom in front of the hotel.

Driving was becoming more of a strain with every
season. It wasn't only the bursitis; now his eyes had
begun betraying him, allowing things to appear suddenly
in front of him with no warning of their approach from
the side.

Ought to get over and get them glasses changed, he
thought. But he knew he wouldn't make an appointment
with an optometrist, or if he made it he wouldn't keep it.
It had been that way all his life. Just the fact of having to
be at a certain place at a certain time was enough to
make him rebel against being there, no matter how important it might be that he go.

Henry's sixty-eighth birthday had passed unnoticed
a few weeks before. His hair was white and full, his skin
pink. In recent years he had begun getting heavy, but the
front-side bulge of his shape was compensated by his increasingly rounded back, so that in profile he appeared
to be straight up and down in front and curved in back,

14

like an archer's bow. The hang of his bib overalls added to the illusion.

This afternoon his mood was mixed. He had driven across the river to the Wisconsin side to check on the beds of wild ginseng in the darkly wooded area near Wyalusing Park. The ginseng looked good. As far as he could tell, no one else had discovered it yet. Another week or so and it would be ready to dig. His yearly ginseng harvest, along with slim Social Security checks, was Henry's only source of income, and in recent years, with more people living in the area, there was a growing danger of his ginseng beds being discovered and pillaged by youngsters or weekend herb-hunters out for a good time and a little easy money. Over the years Henry had become crafty, almost fanatical, about covering his tracks when he went to the ginseng beds, but still he lived with the fear of one day finding them dug over and ruined.

This afternoon his general pre-harvest depression was increased by the fact that it was Friday. That meant an evening at home alone, while the hotel bar was filled with the dress-up crowd. He had long ago decided that on Friday nights it was easier to forgo the silent communion of the bar than to go and sit among the young farmers and miners, out with their wives for some Friday night relaxation.

"Hi, Henry," they'd say, and maybe pat him on the back as they passed. Or, "How's the ginseng look this year?" Then, while he was warming up to answer them, they'd be calling to one another across the horseshoe bar, with old Henry the farthest thing from their minds.

As he neared home, he slowed the car and beeped at a figure standing in the middle of the road. It was the Short boy. Bobby. The boy stepped aside, turned, and

15

sent Henry a smile with such warmth and sparkle that for an instant it penetrated Henry's automatic defenses against the children of Buck Creek.

"Nice day, isn't it?" Robert called above the noise of the car.

Henry's face relaxed into a near-smile. He lifted his head in greeting and agreement, and then forgot the boy in his concentration on driving. The turnoff leading down across the tracks to his house was sharply curved. He swung out wide, aimed the car toward the downhill track, and moved his eyes back and forth until he was sure the road was where it appeared to be, but he didn't let out his breath until the car had safely come to rest beside the house.

He went inside and opened the kitchen cupboard. "Corned-beef hash, Spam, meatballs," he mumbled. "Spam, I guess." He brought down the can and began to open it. Henry's system of meal planning was elementary. Coffee and fruit for breakfast, coffee and a canned vegetable for lunch, coffee and canned meat for supper. That way, he figured, the end result was a more or less balanced diet, with a minimum of bother and dirty pans.

He did all of his living in the downstairs room of the house; it made him feel a little less guilty about living there at all. In the upstairs room were stored all of Harold's clothes and belongings, carefully packed away by Henry after his friend's death two years ago.

The downstairs room was square and airy. Even now, in the afternoon shadow of the bluffs, the half-circle windows filled the room with cool blue light. They looked out over the river, upstream, downstream, and straight across toward the islands and the distant Wisconsin bluffs.

16

Henry brought his coffee and plate of Spam to the TV tray by the big chair, where he ate most of his meals. The meat wasn't warmed clear through, but he didn't notice. It seemed to him that every time he sat in this old chair he sank down deeper and had a harder time getting up out of it. And the house. Every time he had to go someplace it was harder to leave it. When he got home again, he just wanted to stay burrowed in here. Like an old bear in winter, he thought, smiling a little.

The room grew dark. He shifted the tray away from his legs and leaned back into the sagging softness of the cushion behind him.

His eyes stared, unseeing, at the wall. His thoughts were old ones, often replayed. "If Harold was still here, it'd be all right." He didn't realize he was speaking aloud. "As good a friends as Harold and me was, he would have wanted me to come here and live. He was always saying that boardinghouse was no way for a man to live, no cooking privileges or nothing. Harold probably would have left the house to me in his will, if he'd of any idea his time was so near gone.

"That Harold. He was a good friend to me, all right, all right. Never tried to horn in on my ginsenging; never tried to get nosy about my personal life. I sure do miss that old Harold. I told him and *told* him he ought not to drive over that ice yet. I knew it was rotten under the snow. He could've walked out ice-fishing and been okay, but I knew, just as sure as the world, that river wasn't ready for no car to drive over it."

His anger rose, then subsided in futility. The bursitis was a dull ache now, across his shoulders and down into his chest. "Maybe I've got a heart attack coming on," he mused. "Old fool, got nothing better to do than set around worrying about your insides. Ought to have a bullet between your eyes like an old horse that don't die when it's work years is over." But he smiled and snorted a little to himself and turned his mind to the day's findings.

"That Wyalusing bed looks to be worth two, maybe three, thousand this year, if nobody finds it. Down to Sny Magill I should be able to get a few hundred dollars' worth out of there, maybe a thousand. Ought to go take a look at that tomorrow. No, tomorrow's Saturday. Too many kids running around on a Saturday. Next week one day, I'll go down that way."

His mind, drifting back over the day, focused for a moment on the memory of the young Short boy standing in the road, turning to smile in through the car window at Henry. Superimposed over this fresh picture was an older, but equally clear, memory of Bobby Short reflected in the rearview mirror of Henry's car. That was a much smaller Bobby—so small, in fact, that he seemed dwarfed by the spread of his bicycle's handlebars. The boy had hidden beside the road halfway up the Buck Creek hill, waiting for Henry to drive by, and then had followed the car for a little distance, straining valiantly to pump up the hill fast enough, pulling from side to side against the handlebars until finally Henry's car crested the long hill and disappeared.

Henry chuckled now at the memory. "That little bugger sure did want to find my ginseng beds that year. He had them two little girls following me ever'where I went all summer. Couldn't hardly go down to the store for a loaf of bread without tripping over one or the other of them kids."

The thought pleased him, made him feel, in some way, important.

3

Robert was late for supper. After Silent Henry's car passed him on the mine road, he had left the road and climbed back through the tangle of trees and vines toward the base of the bluff. Just a few steps were enough to block out the road, the river and the roof of Henry's house, and to enclose him in a dark green forest-room. Even the practical mind of Robert Short responded to the storybook quality of this place. Here the tree trunks were shrouded with vines and the floor was thick with wild flowers, even now in September. In the face of the bluff was a rocky cleft. A narrow waterfall, no bigger around than Robert but nearly ten times as high, shattered down the cleft to become a short-lived stream ending at the river a few hundred yards away.

Robert picked his way up the stream bed to his sitting rock. Here the splash of the water behind him and the dank mossy smell of the rocks worked together to quiet the restlessness of his body and free his mind of everything but the idea.

It was an exciting idea. It tantalized his imagination. All he had to do was apply the RS Theory of Teacher Handling to Silent Henry, and get Henry to tell him where the ginseng grows. It was the third week in September now, so that would mean about two weeks, maybe less, until the ginseng was ripe enough to dig. Then there would be at least two or three weekends before the season was over, and if he knew where to look for the ginseng, he should be able to harvest at least a thousand dollars' worth during those weekends.

The pleasant pain of excitement rose inside him. The idea wasn't a sure thing, but it was more fun that way, more of a challenge. The RS Theory had certainly worked on his teachers. He could think of no reason why it wouldn't work equally well on Henry, and with Henry the stakes were worth the struggle. He would be playing the game, not for better grades with less work, but for money. Lots of money.

He had begun practicing his theory last year at school, and by this year he had it down to a fine science. The theory was simply that each of his teachers was an individual, with human weaknesses and needs. It was just a question of studying, really studying, the man or woman who stood before him in each class, until gradually he began to understand the need behind each of them. From that point it was simply a matter of supplying the need.

For instance, there was Mr. Anderegg, driver's training: young, in his first year of teaching, trying a little too hard to reach his students on a pal level. With him, Robert was quick, relaxed, almost impertinent but not quite, a sharer of jokes, a bright-eyed boy who met Mr. Anderegg's looks directly, as an equal.

Mrs. Grant, who taught government, knew a totally different Robert Short. She was a dour woman nearing retirement age. She taught without imagination and with the knowledge that her students did not like her. Robert Short was the one exception. She looked down into his open face, his clear dark eyes, and she saw warmth, respect. She did not see in Robert's eyes the cool polite disinterest she had become accustomed to after all these years. Here, at last, she knew, was the eager mind hungering for the knowledge she offered. With Robert looking up at her that way, she felt as though she actually was the revered teacher, the molder of young minds, that she had always pretended to herself that she was. It would have been difficult for her to believe that beyond the door of her classroom Robert Short talked about her with the same insolence as her other students.

With each of his teachers there was a touchstone. The geometry teacher and football coach saw Robert as the one boy who remembered and appreciated his brief fame as a college football star. Some teachers appreciated the student who constantly volunteered answers; others considered this a show-off trait and preferred the student who listened quietly and knew the answers even when he didn't raise his hand. Robert knew all of their preferences, and he used them.

Last year it had been a game to him, a bit of acting aimed at improving his already good grades without putting any additional time into studying. But this year it had gone a degree or two beyond acting. With each change of classes he became a slightly different Robert Short. There was an element of genuineness in his performances that sometimes startled him.

From beyond the screen of trees and vines, the sound of several cars bumping slowly along the road caught his attention. The mine workers, going home. He knew his father would be among them, and that if he wanted a ride back to the house he would have to get down there to the road, but he wasn't ready to leave quite yet.

His gaze, coming back to close range from the direction of the road, was caught by a bit of red on the ground near his left foot. He pushed himself up from the rock and bent over the red.

"Well, if that isn't a good sign, I don't know what is," he said under his breath.

It was a plant, just a few inches high. A cluster of red berries at its center was surrounded by five broad leaves.

"Ginseng. I think."

As carefully as possible, he pulled it up. The two-pronged root was smaller than his little finger. He stared at it for a moment, wondering at its value, then dropped the plant into his jacket pocket.

Suddenly it was cool and damp in the shadow of the bluff, and dark. He picked his way down to the road and started home.

His parents had already begun eating by the time he came into the house. The Shorts were the only family in Buck Creek who ate dinner in the dining room instead of the kitchen. Although it actually made little difference to Robert where he ate, it was one of the family habits that made him glad he belonged to this family. It under-scored the subtle separateness he felt from his friends, and this separateness was important to his self-image.

"Gee, thanks for waiting for me," he said with the proper note of flippancy just short of the smart-aleck point. His parents continued to eat.

"Thanks for getting home on time," his father answered. "Where were you? Your mother said you were coming out to the mine to ride home with me. Did we miss each other?"

"I guess we did. Obviously. I was up by the bluffs, poking around, and I got involved in something." He hung up his jacket, then fished the withering plant out of the pocket and showed it to his father.

"Dad, is that ginseng?"

Don Short was a trimly built and neatly groomed man with an air of youth that almost equalled his wife's. They were a handsome couple, and they enjoyed the knowledge of it. Ten years ago, when the Buck Creek Silica Mine was bought out by a large eastern corporation, Don Short had been sent out from Pennsylvania to manage it. Unlike Miriam, Don had made a deliberate effort to absorb the habits and interests of the people around him, so that almost from the first he had been accepted as a good guy, a good sport, a good mine manager. He was better liked than Mim, who still let it be known in small thoughtless ways that she was Pennsylvania, not Iowa.

Don took the plant from Robert's hand and, holding it out away from the table, examined it.

"I think it is, yes. You see, three big leaves with a smaller one on either side, and the cluster of red berries in the middle. And then the divided root. It's too small to be worth much, though. Where did you find it, out along the mine road?"

"Yep, up by Henry's house. I looked all around, but I didn't see any more of it." He sank into his chair and began unfolding his napkin.

Mim cleared her throat, pointedly. When he ignored her, she sang, "Gentlemen don't come to the table with unwashed hands, dear."

Robert got up promptly and went into the bathroom, but he felt a pinprick of anger at her. There was something condescending about his mother's habit of chiding him so cheerfully. Whenever she used that singsong tone, he felt small and foolish.

What's the matter with me anymore? he thought as he massaged the soap under a stream of painfully hot water.

I've probably got the most easygoing, understanding parents of anybody I know, but sometimes they just get on my nerves.

Mim and Don were still talking about ginseng when he returned to the table. Mim was saying, "I imagine anyplace as accessible as the mine road area would have long ago been picked clean of anything as valuable as ginseng. I know you can hardly find any decent mushrooms along there anymore. Do you want white meat or dark, dear?"

"Both please. Dad, do you have any idea what the going price for ginseng is, this year?"

"I heard thirty dollars a pound," his father said. "They were talking about it down at the bar the other night. Of course, that's for dried roots, and it'd take quite a few plants to make up a pound. Were you thinking about doing a little ginseng hunting this fall?"

"Oh, might." He was tempted to tell them his idea, but it needed a little more thinking through first.

"Why don't you get together a group of friends some Saturday?" Mim said brightly. "You could take a picnic lunch and make a day of it. Go over to Bierbaum woods or some place like that. It might be fun."

He felt a flash of exasperation, out of proportion to its cause. It was a dumb suggestion. Bierbaum woods was as accessible and as thoroughly picked over as the mine road bluffs, as far as serious ginseng hunting was concerned. Bierbaum woods was where the old ladies went to pick mushrooms and Mayapple, and where the dating kids went to park, along the network of deserted logging roads. No one with Robert's intelligence would waste time looking for ginseng in there.

Besides, didn't she know he didn't have a "group of friends"? The next thing, she'd be suggesting he take out his little pals Amber and Meredith for a Saturday picnic in the woods.

But he held back his sharp answer. He was beginning to realize that snappishness at mealtime accomplished only one thing. It spoiled everyone's appetite. Besides, they'd just laugh it off as an improbable joke if he tried to tell them he didn't have a group of friends.

"Anything new at school today?" Mim asked.

"Just the usual rotten stuff. Had a surprise test in government."

"How did you do?" his father said, not really concerned.

"Ah, I've got old Granite wrapped around my little finger. I could tell her we lost the Second World War, and she'd believe me. She thinks I'm great." He smirked with exaggerated modesty.

Mim and Don laughed. "That's our humble son," Mim said.

Robert grinned down into his plate, relieved that the bad feeling was gone.

After dinner he spent an hour or so in the basement enjoying the sight of his twenty-one plush-furred chinchillas moving around in their cages, and letting the new babies hop on and off of his out-stretched palm. But it was Friday night and his mind was charged with the excitement of the new idea. His restlessness grew until finally he went upstairs and pulled his jacket out of the closet. He dropped the now-wilted ginseng plant into the pocket and called, "I'm going out a while."

From upstairs his mother called down, "If we're not here when you get back, don't worry. We're going out, too. I don't know where we'll be, for sure, but probably either the Blue Heron or the Steak House if you need us."

"Okay. Behave yourselves now, and drive carefully." Robert's tone hovered somewhere between teasing and mocking. He felt unreasonably freer knowing they would be out for the evening, even though he wouldn't be at home himself.

He went out and stood poised for a moment, his feet curving over the edge of the top porch step. Where should I go? he pondered, and the answer came. I'll see if I can find Henry. Sound him out a little bit. See if I can lay out a plan of siege.

He bounded down the steps and turned toward the hotel.

4

The bar of the Buck Creek Hotel was not the sort of bar to exclude a sixteen-year-old boy. It was not only a bar but also a restaurant, whenever the volume of business warranted heating up the grill; a midday gathering place for the women of the town; an afternoon gathering place for the school children of all ages; and a parking place for a couple of pre-schoolers whose mothers tended bar and waited on tables. Except for the summer months, there was rarely a time when everyone in the bar did not know everyone else, and the occasional strangers who did happen along were quickly included in whatever conversation was in the air around the horseshoe bar.

Tonight there were the usual Friday-nighters, mostly young couples warming up for the drive to Dubuque or Prairie du Chien for dinner and dancing. Robert greeted them with a casual, all-encompassing wave as he fished a can of pop from the cooler and paid for it. His gaze swept the room. Three men and one of the waitresses were playing euchre at the far side of the room. Amber and Meredith stood with their backs to him, their heads bent over the jukebox in studied ignorance of Robert's presence.

Silent Henry Leffert was not there.

He must be at home then. Guess I'll try there, Robert

thought. He felt reluctant to go to Henry's house. Neither he nor anyone else he knew had ever been inside the little brick house, even before Henry had moved in, when it still belonged to Harold Jones. Of course they had peeked in all of the windows they could reach, during the few days after Harold's death while the house was empty. But going there now, at night, for the deliberate purpose of making friends with an odd old guy whom he really hardly knew, that prospect made even Robert Short hesitate for a moment.

But only for a moment. Then he was walking up River Road, past his own house and on into the darker wooded stretch. His pop can was empty now. He carried it for a while without feeling the cool weightlessness of it in his hand. Then, as Henry's house came into view, he bent the can and pitched it into the river.

I'll ask his advice about something, Robert thought. That's always a good way to start. What does he know about that I could ask about? Ginseng, I guess. That's the only thing I'm sure he knows anything about. I'll tell him I'm writing some kind of a paper, for a school assignment. He'll he flattered. He's bound to be.

Robert felt his way down the embankment in the dark, and stepped over the double gleam of railroad tracks. From the windows of the house came only a dull patch of light. He gathered his bravado and his speech, and knocked.

When Henry opened the door, his face for an instant was blank, as though he couldn't quite remember who Robert was. Spikes of hair stood out from the back of his head, rubbed up by cushion of his chair.

"Hi, Henry. Can I come in a minute?" Robert's face was bright, expectant. He tried to look as though drop-

28

ping in to visit Silent Henry was a common practice of his.

Henry stepped back and, with a mumbled monosyllable, admitted Robert.

"I hope I'm not bothering you, but I was wanting to get some information on ginseng, for a report I have to write for school. So naturally the first person I thought of was you. I figured, if anyone around here knows about ginseng, it'd be Henry. Hey, this is nice in here. I've never been inside this house before, and I always kind of wondered what it was like."

Talking and looking around at the room, Robert stepped into the house and the role. The room surprised him a little. He had expected clutter, odors, perhaps embarrassing signs of poverty. Instead the room, although dim and sparsely furnished, was unusually clean. A TV tray with an empty plate and cup and cutlery were the only objects that even resembled clutter.

Henry motioned to a chair and sat down himself beside the tray. In an instant Robert's attention was fastened on the man across from him. The room's one lamp was so dim that Henry's face was indistinct, but Robert had a sense of both pleasure and constraint in Henry's expression.

For a few moments neither of them said anything. Finally Henry broke the silence. "What did you want to know?" His voice had a faraway quality.

Robert cleared his throat and became matter-of-fact. "We're supposed to write a thousand-word essay on any subject, and since ginseng has always kind of fascinated me, I thought I'd write about it. Can you tell me, well for one thing, what makes it so valuable?"

Some of the constraint eased out of Henry's face. He leaned forward, resting his arms on widespread knees.

"What makes it valuable is them Chinese people. They make ginseng tea out of it. It's supposed to have magic powers, cures about any disease you can think of, makes them feel peppier, things like that."

"Is it really a medicine, then?"

"Hell no, pardon my French. It ain't good for a darned thing. If they get cured, it's all in their heads. But they been using it for millions of years, and you couldn't tell them any different. Not that I'd want to."

Robert nodded thoughtfully. But he wasn't thinking about the Chinese; he was opening his mind and tuning it toward Henry, feeling his way.

"How much would you say ginseng is worth on today's market?" The question had all the detachment of journalistic research.

"Depends."

"Can you give me some kind of a rough average?"

"Maybe twenty dollars a pound, maybe more. I seen it up as high as forty some years."

"How about this year?"

"Hard to say."

Robert sensed a withdrawal and changed courses.

"If it's that valuable, why isn't everybody growing it in his backyard?"

Henry shook his head. "Ginseng don't like to be growed. It wants to choose its own place. Oh, some people's tried raising it as a cash crop, but that domestic stuff don't ever do as well as the wild."

"I see. And what kind of places does it like to grow in?"

"Places where little runny-nosed kids can't find it and pull it all up."

Robert laughed. He wasn't sure whether Henry had intended it as a joke, but he decided to treat it as one, anyway. He laughed and sent a quick twinkling look directly into Henry's eyes.

"Well, Henry, you can't blame a guy for trying, can you?"

For the first time Henry smiled. "Listen, boy, every kid in this country has tried to find my ginseng beds, one time or another. None of them ever did, and none of them ever will."

"No, I guess not," Robert conceded. But when Henry smiled, Robert felt a sure sense of victory. Silently he vowed, You don't know it yet, Henry, but two weeks from now you and I are going to be bosom buddies, out digging ginseng side by side.

He reached into his jacket pocket and fished out the wilted little plant. Holding it out to Henry, he said, "I found that this afternoon, up above the road there. Is it a ginseng plant?"

Henry nodded. "It ain't big enough to be worth anything, though. All this area close to town here had been cleaned out, long since. When I first come up here, these woods was full of it."

Good, Robert thought swiftly. Get the conversation on a personal basis. "You've been here a long time, haven't you? Where did you live before?"

"Ever'where." He spoke curtly; then, somewhat embarrassed, he held the ginseng plant under the lamp. "Look a-here, how this root is broke off. You must have pulled it up, instead of digging. You left half of it in the ground, still."

As smoothly as a chameleon changing colors, Robert moved into a new role. He was a wide-eyed respectful child, eager to learn what the wise old man could teach him. He leaned down close to Henry's head and stared at the severed root.

"Oh, I see what you mean. What is the best way, then, to make sure you get out all the root?"

"Well, I'll tell you, Robert"—Henry's voice expanded as he leaned back in his chair—"most fellows will take some kind of a garden claw to loosen up the dirt, but there's only one kind of digger us professionals ever use, and that's this one here." He held up his hand. "You got to just work down along the stem, feel your way down the root. That's the only way you can be sure you get all them little hair roots. But most fellows don't want to get their hands dirty."

Robert nodded, made a mental note of Henry's disdain for people who won't get their hands dirty, and, with silence and an expectant look, coaxed Henry into talking on.

And talk on, he did. For the next hour Henry talked in an almost unbroken stream. Most of the stories were about things that had happened to people Henry knew, other ginseng hunters, a deckhand on a barge line, a couple of commercial fishermen. He said almost nothing about his own past, nothing that offered Robert any insight into the life of Henry Leffert. At one point Henry rose and made two cups of coffee. He did it with an awkwardness that suggested to Robert that the role of host was a strange one to the man. Although he hated the taste of coffee, Robert accepted the cup and drank it with convincing relish.

As they were finishing the coffee, the already dim light from the lamp between them flickered and nearly went out. When it had settled down again, Robert said, "Are you having power trouble or something?"

"Generator needs looking at. It ain't much good."

"Aren't you on the electric line? It goes by here, doesn't it?"

"It goes by, but I never got around to connecting to it. The generator come with the house, and it does good enough for me."

Robert was puzzled. He was pretty sure it wouldn't cost much to connect the house to the power lines that went by so close to it. Was Henry one of those misers who hoarded every penny? Or was he really so poor that he couldn't afford a little electric bill? Neither possibility seemed logical, when he thought about the money Henry obviously spent on beer in the bar almost every night of the week. But his instincts told him not to pursue the subject.

He stood up, stretching. "Gee, I didn't mean to stay so late. I didn't want to bother you. But this has all been so interesting—"

"Come here a minute. I'll show you something." Henry interrupted so eagerly that Robert sensed, with a flood of hope, that Henry was trying to postpone the leave-taking.

Henry crossed the room to a dresser and took something out of the bottom drawer. Slowly, holding the object cradled in his two hands, he came back into the light.

"Robert, this here is something I don't show around very much, and I don't want the whole town to know I got it. But since you was so interested in ginseng . . . ."

Robert stared down at the object. At first he thought it was a crudely carved doll, but then he saw that it was, instead, a large earth-colored root that had grown in the shape of a man's body. A knob at the top looked surprisingly like a head. Beneath the knob was the carrotlike main trunk, which divided into two leg prongs. Side roots just below the head formed convincing arms that tapered and ended in a fringe of tiny hairlike roots, as did the legs.

"Is that a ginseng root?" Robert asked. For a moment all role-playing v̶   ̶rgotten in his fascination.

"Yep. Ever' onc in a while you'll come across one of these man-shaped r   s, and when you do, it's just like you found the pot of g d at the end of the rainbow. How much would you guess   s here is worth?"

Robert shrugged. "F ty dollars?"

"More like one-thousand dollars." Each syllable was clear and heavy with importance.

"A thousand dollars? Are you serious?" Robert stared down at the root with even greater fascination, and as he did, the head seemed almost to take on features, expression. "What makes it that valuable?"

"Them Chinese is very superstitious about ginseng men, like this here. I don't know if they think it's some kind of god, or what, but for a good one like this they'll pay a lot of money. See, all my ginseng that I harvest, I sell to a fellow down to St. Louis, and he ships it all over to China, and he's always on the lookout for one of these."

"They must be pretty rare, then."

"Oh, hell yes, excuse my French. This is only the third one I ever found, and I been hunting ginseng fifty years. I sold the other two. They was a long time ago."

When Robert finally left and began the dark walk home, his head swarmed with facts and feelings. The facts he filed in the deep recesses of his mind for future use, but the feelings he probed as he walked. Most were vague interwoven impressions of Henry, but there was one impression that overshadowed all the rest. Henry Leffert was a lonely man. Once the initial barriers of strangeness were down, the talk had flowed from Henry like escaping steam. And at the end, he had wanted Robert to stay a little longer.

There was no doubt about it. The siege of Silent Henry was off to a beautifully promising start. Robert had the weapon he needed.

He had uncovered his opponent's weakness.

After the boy had gone, Henry went outside. He walked around to the river side of the house and stood above the concrete retaining wall that separated the lawn from the narrow strip of sandy shoreline. Moonlight shattered over the water, but he didn't see it.

He had a curious feeling of having been painlessly wounded. For a little while tonight, the boy had cracked Henry's carefully built shield of silence. For the first time in years, another human being had come close to his thoughts.

He steeled himself against remembering how exhilarating it had been, just for a few minutes there, to have someone looking at him like that, like he could hardly wait to hear what Henry was going to say next.

Henry shook his head in anger. You old fool, he chided himself. That kid don't care nothing about you. Why should he? He just needed a little information for his schoolwork, so he came here. And you, you open up to him like some crazy old woman, jabbering on and on.

He frowned fiercely into the darkness. And why in the purple blazes did I ever show him my root man? The most valuable thing I own. The only valuable thing I own, the only thing I can count on if I need money in a hurry. An old geezer like me, I could fall and break a hip, be in the hospital for a month, and how would I pay for it if anything happened to that root man? Not that Robert's going to break in and steal it or anything, I don't reckon. But still and all, like I always said, it's best not to tell all you know, or all you got. I won't mention it to him again, and maybe he'll forget about it.

Henry strolled along the top of the low wall for a few yards, then sat down on it, with his feet in the hard ridged sand of the shore.

What makes me think I'd even *have* a chance to mention it to the boy again? he wondered. He got the information he wanted. He won't be coming back for any more visits like we had tonight. A boy like that, he's got more young friends his own age than he'd ever have time for. Girls, too, I expect. He's a charmer all right, all right.

The thought of Robert Short surrounded by his school friends left a rather sad stain in Henry's mind. He could feel a wave of self-pity coming on. For a while he stared out across the broad quiet river at the wooded island far away, near the Wisconsin shore. Tonight everything seemed far away from Henry—everything that, in a vague way, he longed for.

At last he got up and went into the house. He took off his clothes and stretched out on the bed. The moonlight on the waves outside was reflected in moving ripples of light on the ceiling over his bed. He watched it, and listened to the new kind of silence the boy had left behind him.

Out of the silence came softly unsettling memories. For the first time in months, Henry thought about Ruth; for the first time ever, he admitted to just a hint of remorse about what had happened between them. And what had not happened.

5

The next morning, as he always did on Saturday mornings, Robert worked in the chinchilla room. Besides doing the daily chores, he swept and mopped the floor, scrubbed all the water bottles, removed the dust-bath pans from each cage and cleaned and replenished the powder-soft gray dust in which the chinchillas rolled to clean their fur. Then, one by one, he brought each animal out, examined it for color purity under the fluorescent light, ran his fingers over back and hips to be sure the plushy fur was not hiding a thin body.

Two animals he saved until last because, in spite of his determination to remain businesslike, Robert had found himself making pets of these two.

Big Mama was nearly the size of a small cat. Her fur was long and sparse and weak, so that it lay flat against her body instead of standing out like a crew cut, as it was supposed to. Her white areas showed a definite and undesirable brownish tinge, and her ears were as torn as an old tomcat's. She would have been put to sleep long ago except for two things—her ability to produce large numbers of babies of a quality considerably better than her own, and her unchinchillalike placid nature. She had a genuine love of being held and carried around.

The second pet, whom Robert had named Ace, was

Big Mama's opposite in almost every way. He was young, compactly built, and beautifully furred. Even under Robert's homemade fluorescent light, the animal showed no trace of dingy coloring in the white bars of his back fur or around the rim of his chalky underbelly. His color was a true slate blue-gray, and his fur appeared to have the bloom of perpetual prime.

Ace and Big Mama had cost Robert a total of ten dollars.

Robert's interest in chinchillas had begun two years ago, when one of the other members of the junior-high swimming team had mentioned that his father raised them. Robert had wangled an invitation to the other boy's home one evening shortly after that, and had spent the whole evening with the boy's father, asking questions and studying the strange little animals whose cages filled half of the family's garage.

From there on, it was easy. He borrowed all the literature he could find on chinchillas. He studied their fine points until he felt confident that he could tell a good chinchilla from a mediocre one. His friend's father, pleased at Robert's interest, invited him to go along one Sunday to the area's annual chinchilla show.

At the show Robert watched until he spotted the man who seemed to have the most authority. During the lunch break he introduced himself to the man, who turned out to be Joe Welsch, president of the Northeast Iowa Chinchilla Breeders Club. Mr. Welsch, impressed by Robert's intelligence and sincerity, found himself saying, "When you get ready to buy your animals, son, you come down and see me. I don't usually sell my good breeding stock, but I like to see young people like yourself getting into the business, and I'll see you get started right."

Six months later, after a profitable summer of working

at the boat dock, Robert, with his father, drove down to Dubuque, where Mr. Welsch lived. Don Short was soon convinced that his son was not dealing with a shyster, and Mr. Welsch was pleasantly impressed with the well-dressed and well-spoken Mr. Short. When Robert began wandering along the rows of cages, pointing out the animals that interested him, Mr. Welsch was further impressed with the boy's keenness.

Robert and Mr. Welsch worked slowly, choosing two unusually good males and four promising young females from large-littering bloodlines. As he moved along the cage rows, Robert's attention was caught by the tremendous size and sleepy appearance of one old female. When he commented on her, Welsch said, "She's big and ugly, but when she was in her prime, there wasn't a female in the place that could match her for production. Tell you what. For another ten bucks I'll throw her in with the deal. Her production's fallen way off now, but you can probably get another litter or two from her. She'll more than pay for herself."

And then, later, when the seven animals that were to be the foundation of Robert's stake in life were stacked in carrying cages near the door, Robert's attention was drawn to an isolated group of cages of what appeared to be spotted chinchillas.

"What are these?" he asked as he went over for a closer look.

"Fur-chewers," Welsch said. He opened a cage door and brought out the animal that was inside.

Now Robert could see that the fur over the hindquarters had been chewed off to half its length. The black outer tip and the white middle part of the fur was gone, leaving only the charcoal roots.

"What makes them do that?"

39

Welsch sighed. "Nobody knows for sure, but just about everybody's got a few chewers in his herd. Sometimes they'll quit if you move them to a quieter place or change their food or some such as that. But most often there's not a thing you can do to cure them. You don't dare breed them because they'll likely pass the habit on to their young. The most you can hope for is to try to get them stopped long enough for the fur to grow in and get prime. Then you can pelt them."

Robert took the chinchilla from Welsch's hands and looked at him more closely. He was young and obviously of top quality, judging from the fur that was left unchewed.

"What are you going to do with this one?"

Welsch shrugged. "Knock him in the head. I don't have enough cage space to mess around with chewers."

Robert thought for a moment. "Could I have him?"

"Sure, if you want him. He's of no value to me. But I wouldn't try breeding him if I were you. You don't want to take a chance of getting a line of chewers started in your herd."

"No, I won't."

As they were winding up the sale, Robert's father said, "Just out of curiosity, if you can get so much more for an animal by selling it live, for breeding, than by killing it and selling the pelt, why do you pelt them?"

Welsch smiled. "Because if it was just breeders selling to other breeders all the time, pretty soon there wouldn't be any garment production. Then there'd be no pelt market at all, and that building full of chinchillas wouldn't be worth the powder to blow it up."

Robert finished his Saturday cleaning and inspecting chores and, with a feeling of pleasure, sat down on the floor in front of the cages for the last examination. The bottom row of four cages was at eye level. He opened one of the doors and put his hand inside, palm up. In a few seconds the former fur-chewer dropped down into the cage from the raised runway behind it.

"Come on, Ace."

With only token hesitation the little animal hopped into Robert's hand. He sat with his back to the boy, nibbling fingernails. For reasons Robert could not even guess, Ace's fur-chewing had ceased with his change of ownership. For several months, with new fur grown in to replace the chewed spots, Ace had been the most perfect animal in the herd. The bottom tier of cages now held not only Ace but three females and seven babies, including yesterday's three.

The oldest babies were four months old. They were as big as a man's fist, and they watched Robert's hand from their cage next door.

Suddenly Ace's razor-sharp teeth nibbled beyond the dead part of Robert's fingernail.

"Ouch. That's flesh and blood you just hit." He tipped his hand, gently dumping the warm weight of the animal.

He opened the next cage and brought out one of the four-month-old babies. Every time he examined one of Ace's babies, he looked with anxiety and completed his examination with relief that as yet there were no dark chewed spots in the baby fur.

Ace the fur-chewer or the sire of the fur-chewing offspring was worthless; Ace, the reformed chewer who did not pass on this trait to his young, was worth at least three-hundred dollars, possibly more if he was in the ribbons at one of this winter's chinchilla shows.

So far, so good, Robert thought as he stood up.

With an absentmindedness that was unusual for him,

he carried an armload of dirty newspapers outdoors and began to burn them. Already he had forgotten about the chinchillas. His mind was back with Silent Henry, and last night's visit.

Something about the whole idea, the planned siege, was faintly disturbing to him this morning. He couldn't quite isolate the uneasiness. It was almost as though something Henry had said or done last night had made Robert unsure that he wanted to go ahead with the idea. But when he tried to remember exactly when he had begun feeling that way, the uneasiness became so elusive that it almost disappeared entirely.

I think I'll tell the folks about the idea, he decided. See what their reaction is. They might think I'd be taking unfair advantage of the old guy, something like that.

As soon as the fire was burned down to a safe point, he went into the house. Both of his parents were at the kitchen table, still in bathrobes.

"Do you have to walk so loud?" Mim said wryly. "Come have another breakfast with us late sleepers."

Robert washed his hands and poured himself a glass of milk. "You guys must have had quite a time last night. I didn't even hear you come in." He straddled his chair.

"You were sound asleep," Don said. "It must have been nearly three by the time we got home." His hair was rumpled, his voice thick, his face somehow older than usual.

Mim looked better. "We fell in with evil companions," she said. "Harrisons and some others. At eleven o'clock they decided we all had to drive down to Dubuque. Fifty miles of hills and curves. Listen, Bobby, when you start drinking and dating, I hope you have better sense than your father."

Don snorted. "Me! You were the one that wanted to

go. I was an innocent bystander. You twisted my arm."

Robert only half listened to their banter. He'd heard it all before. Often.

Finally he interrupted them. "You'll never guess where I spent my wildly exciting Friday night."

"Where?" Mim said. "Honey, reach me the coffeepot, will you? I'm not moving around any more than I have to this morning."

He dismounted from his backward chair and poured coffee for both of them. "Well, you'll be jealous when you hear. You thought *you* were having a gay evening bar-hopping all over the state. *I* spent the evening at the home of Mr. Henry Leffert."

His father laughed loudly; then, wincing and holding his head, he subsided. "What in the name of heaven were you doing out there, drinking up the old guy's beer supply?"

For an instant Robert hesitated. He wasn't entirely sure they would approve of his plan for Henry. On the other hand, it had been a long time since they had disapproved of anything he did, and for reasons he didn't quite understand, he wanted to tell them about the siege.

"No, I wasn't drinking up his beer supply. I'm after bigger things than that." He paused dramatically until he had their full attention. "His ginseng supply."

Mim and Don exchanged a glance that seemed to say, "That's our boy."

Mim said, "I thought you outgrew that idea of trying to follow Henry, when you outgrew your bike."

Looking down his small nose at her, Robert said, "I don't intend to follow him; I intend to psyche him, and I've already made a good start."

"What do you mean, 'psyche him'?" Don said.

"I mean *psyche* him, like I do my teachers." His eyes

43

narrowed to mysterious slits. "I study their personalities till I figure out what makes them tick, and before they know it, they're convinced that Robert Short is the greatest thing since peanut-butter. It's just a simple matter of psychology."

His slitted eyes darted from his father's face to his mother's. Neither showed disapproval, or even reservation, just amused interest.

Mim said, "Well, I can see how a certain amount of psychology might help you stay on the good side of your teachers, but I fail to see how it's going to help you find that old man's ginseng beds."

"And," his father said, "what will you do if you do find them?"

"Oh, Dad, honestly. What do you think I'll do? I'll dig ginseng, of course. You know darn well, if Henry can make enough money to live on every year just harvesting ginseng for those few weeks in the fall, he's got some awfully good beds of the stuff hidden away someplace. I figure, if I can find out where it grows, I should be able to get at least a thousand bucks' worth, afternoons and weekends. I might even skip a day or two of school. It would be worth it."

Don pursed his lips and considered. "One of the men at the mine was telling me one time that he dug two-hundred dollars' worth of the stuff in one afternoon, up on the bluffs above town someplace. So I suppose it is possible."

Mim said, "But I still don't see what makes you think Henry is going to take you into his confidence all of a sudden, when everybody knows what ridiculous lengths he's always gone to to keep his ginseng beds a secret. Margaret told me one time that Henry used to have an old clunker of a car hidden away out in some abandoned

44

barn, and after he'd leave town he'd sneak around and change cars, in case somebody was following him. If you ask me, the old guy's a little bit off, upstairs."

"Well, you just wait and see," Robert said with an enigmatic smile. "When I turn on the old charm, Henry won't have a chance."

He left the table and started upstairs to his room. But at the landing he stopped to listen.

His father was saying, with a low chuckle in his voice, "You know, honey, if anybody can do it, Robert can. I've never seen a kid that could get around people the way he does. He is going to be one heck of a sharp businessman in a few years."

"What do you mean, 'in a few years'?" Mim retorted. "He's already got more salted away in the bank than we had when we got married. Sometimes I feel like I should be getting the grocery money from *him*." She lowered her voice, so that Robert had to lean over the banister to hear. "How did we happen to have such a smart son, anyway?"

With his bedroom door closed behind him, Robert pried off his tennis shoes and settled himself in the exact middle of his bed. Around him were all the books and notebooks he needed for the weekend's homework assignments. His watch said almost eleven o'clock.

I should be able to get most of it out of the way by lunchtime, he thought. He opened his government book to the assigned chapter and began to read, but after a few pages he realized that none of the printed words coming in through his eyes were making it all the way into his mind. He closed the book, with his finger still in it, and lay back to stare at the ceiling.

Something's bothering me. Now, what is it? What have I got to be in such a bad mood about? What's gone wrong

45

this morning? Nothing, that's what. I've got a darn good chance of making a lot of money pretty soon. It'll be fun trying to get around old Henry. A challenge. I don't even have to bother hiding it from the folks. I told them, and they approved. They didn't say one thing about maybe I'm playing a dirty trick on a harmless old guy. All they said was 'Aren't we wonderful parents, to have such a smart little bastard for a son?' Okay, then. If they think it's such a wonderful idea, the siege is on. I'll really go through with it.

Instead of lifting, his depression grew heavier. He didn't understand why he should feel this frustrating need to lash out at the two people downstairs who so obviously loved him.

6

A few hours later Robert sat among the rocks of the stream bed above Henry's house. His dark mood was nearly gone now, dispelled by action. He was eager to get on with the siege, but reluctant to go knocking on Henry's door again with another manufactured excuse. Not two days in a row, not after all these years of living just up the road from Henry and seldom even speaking to the man.

If he'd just come outside, Robert thought as he stared down at the house, then I could slip down onto the road and just happen to be walking by, on my way out to the mine maybe.

He was in luck. Before he'd even had a chance to become uncomfortable sitting on the damp rocks, a pickup truck rattled up the road and swung down across the tracks and into Henry's yard. Almost immediately Henry emerged from the house. Robert watched with interest as Henry and the driver of the truck lowered its tailgate and began heaving bales of straw out onto the ground. When they were through, Henry counted some money into the driver's hand, and the truck rattled away.

"Don't go back in the house," Robert breathed as he began working his way, with the stealth of an Indian, down the slope to the road. He emerged, caught his breath, brushed himself off with a few hurried swats at his pants and shirt, and started up the road. His thumbs were hooked through his belt loops; his mouth was pursed in a tuneless whistle. He was a study in nonchalance.

Henry was standing beside the pile of straw bales, looking down at it.

"Hi, Henry," Robert called down from the road. He paused, as though trying to decide whether or not to go on up the road, then turned and came down the embankment toward Henry. "What's the straw for?"

"To pack around the pump house, for cold weather," Henry said. His voice betrayed neither pleasure nor displeasure at Robert's appearance.

Robert glanced from the bales to the pump house at the far end of the yard. "Want some help? I don't have anything else to do this afternoon."

Henry shrugged. "Can if you want." He stooped to pick up a bale, but the pull of it against his shoulder made him suck in his breath with pain.

Robert saw, and started to say something sympathetic, then stopped himself. Henry might be one of those persons to whom any acknowledgement of physical pain is a sign of weakness, Robert thought. As casually as he could, he said, "Why don't I carry them over to the pump house, and you can be breaking them open, over there?"

Henry rubbed his shoulder and nodded. "This damned bursitis, pardon my French. There ain't nothing in the world more painful than bursitis." He walked slowly toward the pump house.

Robert followed even more slowly, unbalanced by the weight of the straw bale. The baling wire cut into the palms of his hands, but in his elation he didn't notice.

Talk about luck, he thought. Here's a job I can help Henry with, one he really *needs* help with. And it's a chance to show him I don't mind getting my hands dirty. That ought to score a point or two in my favor. Also, one more little bit of information. Henry likes to talk about his aches and pains. I'll have to remember to be sympathetic.

When all the bales had been moved, Robert and Henry worked side by side, snipping the baling wire, packing mounds of straw around the foundation of the tiny building and weighting them down with strips of tarpaulin and boards. Then they worked inside the pump house until the motorized mechanism in the center of the building was thoroughly insulated from the coming cold.

As they worked, they talked, or at least Robert talked.

"Is this a pretty good well you have here, Henry?" Robert asked.

"It's all right for washing, but it ain't safe to drink. It's too low. Gets seepage from the river."

"Oh. Here, let me take that." Robert relieved Henry of the bale he was trying to lift. "What do you do for drinking water, then?"

"Drink beer."

Robert laughed, assuming Henry had meant it as a joke. For a moment Henry's face was expressionless; then it cracked into a smile, and the two of them were laughing together. In the moment of warmth that followed, Robert risked a more personal remark.

"It sure was nice of Harold to leave his house to you when he died. You two must have been pretty good friends."

Henry turned away and began packing straw around the pump's engine casing.

Robert stood in the narrow doorway of the pump house and gazed out thoughtfully at the little brick house and the river so close behind it.

"This place must be pretty valuable, being riverfront property. My dad says that nowadays, with all the boating and so many people being able to afford summer places, he says any riverfront property around here is a valuable piece of real estate."

Henry's voice had a muffled quality when he answered. "Not this place. It ain't got electricity or drinkable well water, and it floods every year. It ain't worth anything."

Again Robert sensed the man's withdrawal, so he changed the subject. "How come you never got married, Henry? Not that it's any of my business."

"No, it ain't."

Dead end.

"Well, the only reason I asked was that I've often thought I'd like to stay a bachelor all my life, you know, live like you do out here. But, I don't know, I get lonesome sometimes"—covertly he glanced at Henry, who was still looking the other way—"and I just sort of wondered if you ever wished you had a wife to keep you company."

"Nah." Henry stood up and moved slowly past Robert and across the yard toward the house. Robert followed.

They went into the house. For an awkward moment Robert felt that Henry was waiting for him to go. He considered leaving, but he hated to give up his toehold. Only a week or two remained until the ginseng would be ready to harvest; so little time to convert this often-distant stranger into a confidant. And there was no telling when he might have another excuse to come over here.

So he made himself blithely unaware that Henry was standing near the door, a pillar of reluctant hospitality. Robert straddled the arm of the sagging davenport and directed the beam of his appeal toward Henry.

"Sometimes I get so lonesome for someone to talk to, I mean really *talk* to, that I go down in the basement and talk to my chinchillas. Did I tell you I raise chinchillas?"

Henry shook his head and came over to lower himself into the big chair, while Robert told him about the chinchillas. By the time the story was finished, Henry seemed to have relaxed in the enjoyment of listening without having to worry about talking himself.

"Them chinchillas must be awful valuable animals," Henry said when Robert finally ran down. "What are you going to do with all that money?"

Careful now, Robert thought. I don't dare sound greedy. "I'll tell you, Henry, the way I figure, the most important thing for a man to have is his independence, like you've got here. And the only way to be independent is to have enough money to live without having to punch a time clock and waste the best part of your life working for some other guy. So all I'm trying to do is lay up enough of a grubstake so when I get out of school I can travel around a little, try to find something I want to do with my life that will give me the kind of independence you've got, Henry. You may not know it, but you've been a big influence on me."

He stopped to let that sink in.

"Ah, you don't want to be an old bum like me," Henry said, obviously pleased. "You want to go to college, make something of yourself."

"You didn't go to college," Robert persisted, "and I can't think of anyone I know who leads a better life than you do. Have you always been a ginseng hunter?"

He half expected Henry to retreat from this probing, but the man was warm and pink from the rays of Robert's admiration.

51

"Listen, boy, I've done just about everything there is to do. Course, I've always hunted ginseng off and on, but I commercial-fished, I clammed, I worked on the barges and in the button factory. I even farmed for a while, when we was living down by Bellevue."

He faltered for an instant, then hurried on, as though he were afraid Robert might interrupt. "But I finally come to my senses and decided ginsenging was the only way to live. Why, Robert, I've slept more nights on the ground than you have in a bed."

"Do you camp out when you're digging your ginseng?" Robert was all eager intensity.

"Not anymore, but I did when I was younger. Covered more territory then. Now I just work the places that are close to home."

Robert held his breath.

"I remember one time, years ago . . ." Henry launched on a series of reminiscences, and Robert ceased holding his breath. There would be no hints from Henry as to how close to home his ginseng beds were.

7

It was Saturday night and the bar of the Buck Creek Hotel was thick with smoke and noise. The Saturday-night people consisted mostly of middle-aged farmers from near Buck Creek, most of them without their wives. They were older and not so dressed up as the Friday-night customers, and Henry felt more comfortable in their presence.

He sat at his accustomed table in a corner of the room near a window, where he could look either at the room full of humanity or at the glittering black river beyond the window. His beer sat untouched at his elbow. He didn't really feel like drinking it, but it was necessary to buy something, to be a paying customer. It was the price of admission to the fellowship of men.

The noise eddied around him but did not penetrate his solitude. He neither spoke to the others nor heard what they said, and yet he absorbed comfort from the fringes of their company. He knew that the barrier of silence between him and the others was of his own making, a shield to hide all the small ugly truths of Henry Leffert. It was necessity, but on nights like tonight it was a burden to him.

All that talk this afternoon, he mused. Kind of give me the taste for talking again, I reckon. I ought not to let that boy hang around. He's after something, and he don't need to think he's fooling me that he just comes around because he likes my company. He'd like to know where them ginseng beds is, more than likely. Well, so would a lot of people, but old Henry ain't feebleminded. Not yet.

For a moment he smiled. It warmed him to know that he was a town character, that the children schemed to find out something that only he knew, that when Buck Creek people had visitors from out of town, Silent Henry, the ginseng man, was one of the picturesque highlights of the sight-seeing. He recognized the fact that a big part of his legend was the well-guarded secret of where his ginseng grew, and that without the legend he was no more interesting than Grampa Severs or any of the other colorless old men of Buck Creek.

That boy don't need to think he's fooling me, Henry said again to himself. But Henry wasn't thinking about Robert's motives for establishing a friendship. He was thinking of the boy's bright, open face smiling up at him. He was remembering as much as he could of the things Robert had said.

"I'd like to stay a bachelor all my life, you know, live like you do."

"I get lonesome sometimes . . ."

"Did I tell you I raise chinchillas? . . . I want the kind of independence you've got."

"I just sort of wondered if you ever wished you had a wife to keep you company."

A wife to keep me company, Henry thought. Suddenly Ruth's face was clear in his mind, the way she'd looked that last day.

It was in midsummer of 1947 or '48. Henry could

never remember exactly. He and Ruth were renting a little place on the river near Bellevue, where Henry and another man kept seine nets in the backwaters and caught rough fish in commercial quantities. In the fall he always took a couple of weeks off from the nets to dig ginseng.

Henry was taller then, more tanned and hardened, and it pleased him to know that women considered him handsome, maybe even a little dangerous. He believed that Ruth was lucky to have caught him when she was young and good-looking, when he had not yet reached his prime, because by now the balance was greatly in his favor.

Ruth, by that time, was shapeless, colorless, almost featureless with middle age. She was good-natured enough most of the time, at least when other people were around, but lately Henry had begun feeling toward her the way he used to feel toward his mother when he was young. It was as though Ruth had set herself above him as a self-appointed keeper of his conscience. She felt that it was her right and duty to keep track of what he did and where he went. To her, this was only natural, and any wife who didn't do the same was a fool.

It seemed just as right and natural to Henry, then, to avoid telling her the truth as much as possible. If he wanted to go up to Dubuque to buy some new lead weights for his nets, he told Ruth that he was going to Clinton on business that didn't concern her. If his ginseng check totaled twenty-three hundred dollars, he told her it was eighteen.

As time went on, he began to resent having to support someone whose only aim in life was to slow down his fun. She's an able-bodied woman, he reasoned. Why should I knock myself out working twenty-four hours a day just so she can spend it all?

The situation came to a head on that summer afternoon of '47 or '48. It was not so much *what* Ruth said as he started out the door after lunch, as it was the fact that she said it every time he started to leave. "Where are you going? Why? When will you be back?"

This time, when she asked, her words, her tone, the very pressure of her watchfulness against his freedom, made something inside him suddenly let go.

"I'm going to hell on a pink pig and I'll see you when I see you!"

He slammed out the door and, wrapped in self-righteous fury, marched down to the river's edge. As he loosed the big old flat-bottomed fishing boat and pushed it away from his handmade dock, he told himself it would serve her right if he just went off someplace and stayed a few days. Let her stew a while. Maybe she'd appreciate him more if she had to do without him for a week or so.

He took the time to empty his seine nets and the few hoop nets he had staked out in the backwater. Then, with a boat full of fish and nets and a spirit light with the joy of truancy, he started upriver.

The fish brought enough at Dubuque to buy food, beer, and gas for the boat. In a general way his plan was to keep going, just poking along at his own speed, until the food and money were gone, or until he felt like going back home.

The food and money ran out at Buck Creek, and because he still felt no particular desire to face Ruth just yet, he stayed. He took a room in a boardinghouse and began exploring the river for good seining spots. In the bar one night he saw Harold Jones, who worked for the railroad and had sometimes laid over in Bellevue, where he and Henry had got to know each other in a casual way. He asked Harold not to mention around Bellevue that he had seen Henry in Buck Creek. "My old lady's on the warpath," he explained. "She gets some funny ideas sometimes. You know women."

The days and weeks slipped past almost unnoticed. Fishing was good around Buck Creek, and when ginseng time came, early in October, he found lush pockets of it along the bluffs. Still he felt no compelling urge to go back to Bellevue.

Henry lived one day at a time, seldom planning ahead or looking back. He was content being where he was, doing what he was doing. His life force was inertia. At some point during the winter he began to think of Buck Creek as home, and of Ruth and Bellevue as part of another existence.

Occasionally he missed her. Occasionally he caught himself talking to her in his mind, saying, "Gonna be a cold one today, with that wind out of the north." Or, "Where did I put them toenail clippers?" But since the thought of Ruth brought guilt, and therefore resentment, he chose not to think about her very much. The people he met in Buck Creek assumed he was a bachelor. He never told them anything different.

Months became years. He no longer thought about going back. He ceased wondering how Ruth was getting along, how she was fixed for money. Eventually he gave up the winter part of his fishing. Ice fishing was just too much trouble. Too uncomfortable. Instead he spent more and more time exploring the islands and the less accessible wooded areas along the river, looking for the places where the ginseng grew, marking them in his mind so that he wouldn't have to waste time in haphazard searching during the short harvesting season.

When Henry had been in Buck Creek for more than ten years, Harold Jones retired from the railroad and bought the oddly shaped pink brick house on the mine road. The two men became friends, although Henry avoided talking about Bellevue. Sometimes when Henry was having a slim year, Harold invited him to come and stay at the pink brick house for a while, until fishing picked up or until the yearly ginseng check allowed Henry to pay what he owed at the boardinghouse and move back to his room there.

After Harold's car went through the ice, after the funeral service was over and the last of Harold's few relatives were gone, Henry decided it was wasteful to pay fifteen dollars a week at the boardinghouse when that perfectly good house of Harold's was standing empty. So he moved in.

He assumed some relative had inherited the house and would be along any day to claim it. When that happened, Henry planned to vacate graciously, saying that he'd just been keeping an eye on the place for his old friend.

That was two years ago. As yet no one had come to claim the house, although Henry realized that somebody must be paying the taxes. He kept the house neat, much neater than he would have otherwise, so that the owner might be less angry when he finally came and found Henry living there.

Someone in Buck Creek had surmised that Harold must have willed the property to Henry. Since Henry didn't deny it, the surmise was accepted as fact.

But Henry didn't feel right about it. It was something else he didn't want people to find out about, something else to guard against in casual conversation. He had an uneasy feeling that what he was doing was illegal, just as he was afraid that if Ruth found him she could have him thrown in jail for desertion or whatever the charges would be.

It was fear of exposing himself that eventually caused him to talk less and less, when he sat around the bar in the evenings. He had no close friends now. He didn't dare to.

Gradually he became aware of the familiar smoky room around him. The jukebox drowned out the television set above the bar, but it couldn't drown the voices of the men.

"How's your corn look this year, Harley?"

"Awful wet yet. It tested out way over twenty-five. Looks like I'll be out there picking corn Christmas day."

"Many's the time I've picked corn on Christmas."

"Harley, you ought to sell out, move in to town, and make your ol' lady go to work. How 'bout that, Edna?"

And Edna answered, "If I have to go to work and earn it, then *I* get to spend it. I'll cut him off at the pockets, and see how he likes it."

Laughter. Another round of drinks.

Henry listened to them, and as he did, he heard another voice. "I'd like to have the independence you've got, Henry. You may not know it, but you've been a big influence on me . . . Sometimes I get so lonesome for someone to talk to, I mean really *talk* to . . ."

He clenched himself against the thought of the boy.

8

The whispering sound of rain on the river water woke Henry. It was Monday morning. "Blue Monday," he mumbled as he lay there waiting for some necessity to rouse him from the bed. Nothing to do today, he thought. No point in taking the risk of driving anyplace to check ginseng. Not with these eyes acting up. Guess I'll clean house a little this morning, dust off Harold's things upstairs.

Through the steady sibilance of the rain came another sound, a soft gnawing.

Mice again, he told himself. Cold weather coming on. I better put out traps. They can do a lot of damage to a house. If the owner showed up and found the place full of mice . . .

Slowly he rolled up out of bed and started the fire under the coffeepot. The action brought back into his memory the picture of Robert standing there Saturday afternoon waiting for the coffee to perk, getting down the cups. Henry sighed, and the depression he had felt last night came back.

Not that I really expected him to come again yesterday, he told himself. The only thing about it, I just thought because it was Sunday, maybe he wouldn't have nothing better to do, and he might have stopped by.

Hell, if he's trying to find out where my ginseng is, he ain't got much time to waste.

He poured his cup of coffee and took it to one of the rounded windows overlooking the river. Leaning against the sill, he watched the raindrops shattering the surface of the river until the steam from his coffee blurred the scene outside.

Maybe what I should have done, last time he was here, maybe I should have acted more like I *might* tell him where it grows. That way, he'd be sure and come back to work on me some more. Maybe he got discouraged. Or maybe that ain't what he's after at all.

He sighed again. Yes, it is, Henry. No use being more of a fool than you have to. That is one boy that don't ever waste any time just being chummy.

It was late morning when Henry heard a car coasting down across the tracks and into his yard. He was upstairs, passing a dustrag over the cartons of Harold's belongings. At the sound of the motor outside, he went to a window and looked down. It was a stranger, a well-dressed businesslike man slamming the door of an expensive-looking car.

Panic held Henry at the window, but his eyes went out of focus.

This is it, he thought, catching and holding his breath till it pained him. This is the end, what I've been afraid of all along. They're coming to get the house.

His heart was pounding as he descended the narrow stairway. The man was knocking at the door now. After the first squeeze of panic Henry felt a lightness, almost relief. It's all over, but anyway I don't need to keep on being afraid it might happen, he told himself. He opened the door.

"How do you do. I'm sorry to bother you." The man

was smiling pleasantly through the waterfall of rain that spilled from the rim of his hat. "Would you mind if I step inside for a minute?"

Henry moved aside and allowed the man to come in. He wondered why the man was being so polite, why he hadn't demanded to know what Henry was doing living in his house.

"My name is Ralph Jester, from Iowa City. I was just driving around, sort of keeping an eye open for some riverfront property that might be for sale, you know, for a vacation home. I saw this house, and I just thought I'd stop and find out whether it might be for sale, by any chance, or maybe available for a long-term lease. Do you own the place?"

Henry stared, as the man's words echoed through his mind. It wasn't all over, after all. Part of him rejoiced that he still had a home, while another part of him sighed and reassumed the burden of the deception.

"The house ain't for sale." He nearly pushed the man out into the rain, ignoring the look of surprise and offense on the stranger's face. He fixed himself another cup of coffee. His hands shook with delayed tension.

If that really had been the owner, he thought slowly, and he was coming to kick me out, the story would be all over Buck Creek before suppertime. Crazy old Henry Leffert has been living in Harold's house all this time under false pretenses. Ain't no way on God's green earth that a story as good as that could keep from getting all over town. If they laughed at me before, what would they do then?

An ache was starting in his shoulder, and down through his chest, as he imagined what Robert would think, if he knew. That boy would sure as hell never want anything more to do with me if he knew. I wouldn't be no influence on his life then, like he was saying. He probably didn't mean it, but on the other hand maybe he does admire me a little. Well, he wouldn't if he knew about me, that's for sure.

He set his cup down, with a little clattering noise. His hand still shook. Bending down on one stiff knee, he dragged open the bottom dresser drawer and took out the root man. He held it to the gray watery light from the window, and felt the weightlessness of it.

A thousand dollars I could get for this. Enough for a room at the boardinghouse for quite a while, if worst comes to worst. I won't sell it unless I have to, but if they take my house away from me . . . As he hid the root under a flannel shirt and closed the drawer, he felt somewhat better.

After lunch, when the rain had stopped, he filled a cardboard carton with dirty laundry and drove, very cautiously, up the mine road to the hotel. He carried the box through the back door and down to the laundry room in the basement, where there was one coin-operated washing machine and dryer for the convenience of the families who parked their trailers in the lot behind the hotel in the summertime, and for the few old people around town who had no washing machines of their own.

When his clothes were clean, dried, and neatly folded back into the carton, Henry went around to the front of the hotel. Tom and Grampa Severs were at their post. They moved their canvas chairs to make room for him, but Henry just waved and went on. Sometimes he liked to sit with them, but more often, as now, the two old men depressed him. They were much older than Henry, both in their eighties. He didn't like their monotonous complaining or their dull talk about when they were young.

I'd rather have youngsters around me, any day, he told himself as he ambled across the tracks to the little riverside park. That wasn't strickly true. He didn't particularly enjoy children either, but he knew that in the eyes of the children of Buck Creek, Silent Henry was a fascinating character who knew a tremendous secret—where the ginseng grows—and in their own way they looked up to him. It was more than he got from the adults around town, and he enjoyed playing the role, even though the children themselves often irritated him.

He veered along the tracks and angled down to the little wooden bait stand. At the battered pop machine beside the stand, he fished two dimes from his pocket and slid out a bottle of pop. A beer would have been more to his liking, but Tom and Grampa Severs were drinking beer, and right now he felt more like aligning himself with youth than with old men gossiping in the sun. Besides, Tom and Grampa had each other. They didn't need his company.

The clock inside the bait house said a little after three o'clock. Henry went down to the shore and sat on a swirl of roots at the base of one of the huge old trees that grew at the water's edge. But he didn't look out toward the water. He sat facing the hotel corner where the school bus would be unloading before too long.

If he don't happen to notice me and come over for a little visit, Henry thought, I won't call out to him or nothing like that.

But in his mind he was seeing Robert alighting from the bus, looking happy to see Henry, coming over to drink a bottle of pop with him. They'd sit there with their backs against the tree trunk, and just look out over the water, sort of dreamy, and not be in any hurry to go anywhere.

Maybe he'd like to hear my story about that time Harold and I went frogging and damn near got run down by the barge, thought Henry. That's a pretty good story. Or maybe he'd like to know some more about ginseng, or I could tell him all about mushrooms. Nobody around here knows mushrooming like I do.

He closed his eyes and smiled.

As the school bus coasted down the hill into town, Robert was congratulating himself on having had the will power to stay away from Henry all day yesterday. It hadn't been easy, a whole empty Sunday and Henry just a half-mile up the road, but his instinct told him not to push.

But what now? he thought. I don't have time to play hard to get for very long. Maybe tonight I can think of some excuse to go up there, or maybe Henry will be in the bar, and I can accidentally run into him there. Let's see now, I'll be sure to ask him how his bursitis is, and I'll be very sympathetic when he tells me about his aches and pains. Maybe I should give him a little more of that bit about my not having any friends. I think that hit home with him.

When the bus stopped, he was deep in thought as he pulled himself out of his seat and followed Amber up front toward the door. She said something to him, but he didn't listen. He grunted something noncommittal, and she turned away.

As he jumped down from the bus, he saw Henry sitting against a tree, down by the water. Luck, luck, luck, Robert sang silently. Boy, I must live right. I'll just swing on down there, and we can sit and talk and be big old buddies.

As he started toward Henry, Robert realized with a small jolt of surprise that, all maneuvering aside, he really was glad to see the old guy.

After this is all over, he thought, I actually believe I'm going to miss talking to Henry. I don't suppose he's going to be much of a buddy after the siege.

Robert grinned, but there was something stiff and uncertain about the grin.

9

It was Thursday afternoon. The sixth-period P.E. class, divided into the Reds and the Blues, was playing itself on the basketball court. Because there was no visible way of telling a Red from a Blue, occasionally a player passed the ball to a member of the opposing team without realizing it until the damage was done.

Robert stood close beside his guard, watching Mr. Harmon prepare for a jump ball. He felt no weariness, just a panting, tense kind of excitement. He felt like steel and clockwork. If the ball came anywhere near him, it would automatically be drawn into his hands, and from there it would soar through the hoop as though it were guided by radar. He felt slim and hard and fast and unconquerable.

The two jumping players were in position now, half crouched, staring up at the ball Mr. Harmon held above them. While his guard was watching the two jumpers, Robert eased over and back a few steps, then moved around until he was in the clear.

The whistle blew. The ball was in the air. The jumpers shot up after it, and it was tipped in Robert's direction.

He darted to meet it. Bending low under the flailing arms of his guard, he pivoted and raced toward the far end of the court. For an instant there was nothing before him but the varnished gold of an open floor. The ball was alive under his hand. It might have been a Yo-Yo, attached to him by a string.

Then abruptly the way was blocked by hostile Reds. They spread their hairy legs and flapped their arms in his face. The basket was half a floor length away, out of sight behind their bobbing heads.

Robert veered. A Blue appeared, halfway between Robert and the basket. He was close enough to get a fair shot, and he was in the clear. But now, for a split second Robert was in the clear, too. The decision was automatic.

He gathered his steel-and-clockwork muscles, and shot. It was close. The ball brushed the net as it fell short. It landed in Red hands.

For the remaining few minutes of the period Robert avoided his teammates' eyes. He could feel waves of resentment from Gary, the Blue to whom he should have passed the ball.

Finally Mr. Harmon blew his whistle. "Okay, that's it. Reds, twenty-three; Blues, twenty-one. Showers, everybody."

As Robert passed Mr. Harmon, he looked the other way. Mr. Harmon was the one teacher who, Robert suspected, was capable of seeing through him. He remembered with discomfort the talk they had had at the first of the year. Robert had gone to Mr. Harmon and said that he would like to go out for basketball this year. Mr. Harmon's answer came back to him now, as he stood under the shower. "Robert, you're a good enough player, in spite of your size, but I wish you wouldn't try out. Frankly, team sports just aren't your meat. Go out for swimming, tennis, even track if you want to. That's the kind of sport where you can compete as an individual, where you don't have to hold back your personal performance for the good of the team."

He turned his face up into the force of the shower and thought, Well, Harmon, I did it again, didn't I? But I was so sure I could make this shot. And I almost did.

While he was dressing, Gary called across the intervening benches, "Hey, Short, how come you didn't pass to me? I was wide open. Didn't you see me?"

"Yeah, I saw you," Robert muttered, looking down as he buttoned his shirt.

He felt the growing distance between himself and the others. They were all in twos and threes, talking in soft monosyllables or laughing at something Robert couldn't hear. He resented the exclusion. He gathered his books and went outside to wait for the bus. Amber and Meredith sat with their backs to him, on the low retaining wall. Robert looked at them for a moment, remembering how it had been when they were all little kids, best friends, a leader with two devoted followers competing for his attention, even for his mild little-dictator abuse. Like the time he'd handed Amber a large but harmless bull snake, then told her it was deadly poisonous and trained to bite at his command.

He thought about going over and talking to the girls till the bus came. The locker-room snubs still smarted. Amber and Mer aren't much, but at least they appreciate me, he thought. I'll just wander over there, kill a little time with them till the bus comes. Or would that be bad for my image, hanging around with them?

He was still thinking about it when the bus arrived and it was too late. As always, he had the seat over the right rear wheel to himself.

The driver called back, "Is that everybody? Where's—

oh, there she is. Okay, you little monsters, keep it down to a roar." There was a general giggling and subsiding as the bus rolled into motion.

Robert tuned out the noise around him and deliberately turned his mind to the siege. He was pleased with the ground he had gained that week, but he was also a little surprised at Henry's resilience. The old man let him get just so close and no closer.

On Tuesday night he had dropped by Henry's house to borrow a book he'd seen there, *Wild Ginseng and Other Herbs of North America*. They had talked a while. Robert asked how the ginseng looked this year, and Henry said, not bad. Robert said he didn't think there was anything more exciting in the world than hunting ginseng. Henry said nothing.

On Wednesday night Robert returned the book with profuse thanks. In study hall that afternoon he had written an essay on ginseng, an essay in which professional ginseng hunters emerged as a romanticized mixture of Daniel Boone and Johnny Appleseed. The English teacher had given no writing assignment, but he knew she would one of these days, so his work would not be wasted. On Wednesday night when he returned Henry's book, he showed Henry the essay. It was impossible to tell for sure, but Robert had gone home with the definite feeling that Henry had been flattered by it.

And now, Thursday night was coming up. During most of the bus ride home Robert pondered. No, he finally decided as they began the descent into Buck Creek, three nights in a row would be too much.

At dinner that night Mim asked her stock question. "How did it go at school today?"

He didn't want to think about school. Thinking about it brought back his resentment of Mr. Harmon's attitude. His memory blurred the distinct edges of fact, while it swelled his resentment.

"Oh, okay, except Harmon was picking on me again."

"What about?" his father asked with some indignation.

Robert snorted. "He thought I wasn't being a good sport, just because I tried for a long shot when we were playing basketball in P.E. He thought I should have passed to Gary Johnson, because Gary was closer to the basket, but Gary's a rotten shot and I figured we'd stand a better chance with me shooting, even from the middle of the floor. Harmon just doesn't like me. We have a personality clash."

"I think that's terrible," Mim said. "Teachers should encourage the superior students instead of trying to hold them down to the level of the poorer ones, even in sports. That's the trouble with too many teachers nowadays. I'm going to bring this up, next school board meeting."

As he reached for the salad, Don said, "Oh, now, Mim, it's nothing to get in a lather about. Robert's just beginning to find out that the world is full of petty jealousies. When you're a little smarter or more talented or more capable than the people around you, there's always going to be somebody waiting to try to bring you down. You just go right on doing the best you can. Don't pull your punches for anybody. You want to start the bread around?"

Robert felt somewhat soothed, and yet a small part of his mind remained aloof from his parents' judgment. He wanted to be able to accept what they said without questioning it. It would free him from the shadowy suspicion that perhaps Robert Short was not as good a sport as he should be.

His inner voice rose almost to a whine as he thought,

But if parents are supposed to be so all-seeing and all-knowing, why don't they *tell* me if I'm wrong?

He left the table before dessert and went down to the basement. The chinchillas were already fed, watered, and cleaned up after, so he opened Big Mama's cage and put in his hand. With a rolling, lumbering motion the animal came to his hand. Her tattered ears drooped and most of her whiskers were broken off, but her eyes sparkled bright black out of the dingy gray of her face. She examined his hands for possible raisins, then contented herself with nibbling his nails.

After a few moments, when Robert's arm was beginning to ache, she stepped up into his hand and began her awkward climb to his shoulder. Crowding as close to his head as she could, she shifted around until she was facing forward. Then, with a soft sound of contentment she settled down for the ride.

Robert sauntered around the room. He moved carefully so that she wouldn't lose her balance. The incredible softness of her fur filled his ear and sent chills down his back. When he stopped walking for a moment, Big Mama's whiskers brushed across his cheek and nose.

"You like me, don't you, old girl? You don't think I'm a crumby guy. Let's go find you some raisins."

He returned her to her cage, slipped her a few raisins, took a quick look at Ace's babies to assure himself that they hadn't begun fur-chewing, then went upstairs to his bedroom to watch television. His parents were watching the same show on the color set in the living room, but right now he preferred the privacy of his room.

Long after his parents were in bed and the house was black and still, Robert lay across his bed watching without really seeing the television screen. He was still dressed. An irritating kind of restlessness made it im-

72

possible to concentrate on the show or to get ready for bed. Finally he turned off the set and went down the stairs and out onto the front porch.

I feel like doing something, he thought, but what? I feel like talking to somebody. Henry. I really would like to go talk to old Henry for a while, he repeated, with some surprise. But I don't dare show up out there again so soon. Especially not at this time of night.

Even though he knew he wouldn't go to Henry's house, he began walking out the mine road. The action eased his restlessness somewhat.

There was enough of a moon so that Robert could see the rocks and ruts ahead of him. He walked easily, slowly, hands in pockets, savoring his aloneness in the night. The crisp night air held the memory of childhood games played in the giddy after-dark hours—hide-and-go-seek, with Amber usually being It; statues and tag; all the acting games his imagination had provided for the three of them.

Suddenly a floating palace of lights appeared around the point of the long wooded island opposite him. It was the *Casey,* the largest of the towboats that passed Buck Creek. She moved silently up the river, her eight barges merely flat black rectangles on the water in front of her. Occasionally the lights on one of her many decks were blotted out by the moving figures of her crew. Robert waved, even though he knew he was invisible to them.

He remembered when he used to imagine that the *Casey* was a stern-wheeler pleasure boat and he was the diamond-studded gambler, getting ready to board her for the trip to New Orleans.

He watched her slow progress until she was out of sight around the bend; then he resumed the rhythm of his walk. He went past the darkened block of Henry's house; past the mystic ruins of a distillery that had failed around the turn of the century when one of its owners fled to Canada with the company funds; past Angel Falls, slightly larger than the falls above Henry's house; past the cleft in the bluffs that reputedly had sheltered part of a bootlegging operation during Prohibition.

At last the road ended in a Y, under a large sign that said, "Buck Creek Silica Mine—DANGER—No Admittance." The lower branch of the road went down to the railroad tracks, the mine's main offices and loading docks. Robert ducked under the DANGER sign and followed the upper branch. It rose along the face of the bluff and ended at the mammoth gaping entrance to the mine itself.

Robert loved the mine, partly because his father was the manager, which gave him special privileges denied to other Buck Creek children, and partly because of the feeling of awe he always got, looking up at that towering black cavern.

He stood around a while, not doing much of anything except pitching a few rocks and absorbing the spirit of the place; then he started back.

As he walked, he thought about Henry Leffert, not about how best to worm his way into the old man's confidence, but just about Henry himself. What was he like, I wonder, when he was my age? Was he always such an unfriendly person, or did he have some kind of tragedy in his life to make him so untrusting? I wonder what he thinks about me, really.

He kicked a crumpled beer can ahead of him for a few steps, but it made too much noise.

If I told Henry about that basketball game today, he mused, what would he think—that I'm a little fair-haired

74

darling who can do no wrong, or that I'm a spoiled brat?

Funny, the other night when I was giving him the 'poor lonesome me' routine, I told him that when I need somebody to talk to I go down and talk to the chinchillas. I was just making it up, but tonight that was just exactly what I did.

He smiled. His imagination began to write a fable about a boy who told lies, and every lie he told became the truth. Like Midas, a little, he mused.

At the spot where the road looked down over Henry's house, Robert stopped. He sat on a rock at the edge of the road.

Henry's down there sleeping, he thought. I wonder if he'd be mad if I went down and knocked on the door and woke him up. Sure he would. He probably just thinks of me as a pest. I wonder if he does ever think about me when I'm not around. I wonder if I'm making any progress at all with him.

His hands began to break a twig into inch-long segments. The night was so quiet he could almost hear the pulse in his neck and ears.

Inside the house, Henry lay staring out at the sky through his half-circle windows. The room was so dark that he was not aware of how blurred his vision was, every place except straight ahead.

He had been sleeping so lightly that the sound and the lights of the passing *Casey* had awakened him. As sometimes happens, Henry's night thoughts were more honest than those during the day. Painfully honest.

I'm just a worthless old liar, he told himself. It's no wonder I ain't got any friends. Even Harold wouldn't of liked me if he'd known what I done to Ruth. And if there's such a thing as Heaven, and Harold is setting up there watching me live in his house, then I know damn well he's cussing me up one side and down the other. If I died right here tonight, if I had a heart attack and died right now, not one person in this world would care enough to come to the funeral. Ruth must already think I'm dead, after twenty years.

Robert might care, he thought. He might care whether I lived or died. No, who am I kidding? All in the world that boy wants out of me is to find where my ginseng it.

He rolled over on one side.

Maybe that's not all, though. Maybe he really does like hanging around me. It seems like he does, sometimes. He's a likable young kid, the way he looks at me like I was the wise old man of the mountain or some such.

If I did let him in on my ginseng, I wonder what would happen. Would he take so much of it that I couldn't earn enough to live on next year? Would he tell his friends, and they'd laugh at crazy old Henry, and a whole gang of them would go out and ruin my ginseng, so I wouldn't ever have enough to live on, ever again? They could, if they pulled so much that it didn't reseed itself.

If I told Robert where it was, would we be better friends?

A pain settled in Henry's chest.

No, if I told, Robert would never come to see me again. Why should he bother hanging around with an old liar like me, once he's got what he's after?

In the honesty of midnight, Henry faced the fact that the sham companionship of a scheming boy was better, than going back to the echoing silence of his old life.

10

Lack of sleep seldom bothered Robert, but the day after his midnight walk up the mine road he had to fight drowsiness in every class. In government, right after lunch, it was a constant struggle to keep his head from bobbing. He kept his spirits up only by reminding himself that it was Friday; then that it was Friday afternoon; and finally the last class of Friday afternoon.

During the bus ride home he allowed his head to fall back and his eyes to close. He was floating through the numb approaches to sleep when the bus slowed and someone said, "Hey, an accident."

Robert sat up and looked out the window. The bus had just rounded the corner at the top of the two-mile-long Buck Creek hill. In the ditch at the side of the road was an old blue station wagon lying on its side, its grimy chassis exposed.

Robert shot out of his seat. "Mack, stop. Let me out," he called to the driver. He lurched toward the front of the bus, dropping his books in Amber's lap as he went by. "Here, hang onto these for me. I'll get them later."

Mack slowed the bus, looked back dubiously at Robert, then reluctantly applied the brakes and opened the door. "Can you get home all right from here?" he asked as Robert leaped down out of the bus.

"Sure. Go on."

The Highway Patrol car had already arrived, and Robert could see a tow truck coming. He went over to the patrol car. The two uniformed officers stood beside the open back door of the car, where a third man sat with his head lowered over his outspread knees.

Robert greeted the patrolmen with a quick, somber "Hi," then came closer and squatted beside the other man.

"Henry? Are you okay?" Robert looked up at one of the patrolmen. "Is he hurt, Marv?"

"He's just shook up a little bit. He'll be all right."

The patrolmen turned away to talk to the driver of the tow truck.

Henry raised his head and met Robert's worried stare. He didn't say anything, but Robert knew that Henry was glad, very glad, to see him.

"Boy, Henry, you really did it, didn't you? What happened, anyhow? Do you feel okay?"

"Just a little dizzy. Knocked the breath out of me, and I think it wrenched my shoulder some. I feel like somebody pulled my arm right out of its socket. Got a little blood up here." He raised a shaking hand to touch one cheekbone, which had been scraped.

Robert looked at the car. He went over for a closer look and walked around it for a few minutes with the others, studying the best way to get it upright and out of the shallow ditch. By now a handful of cars had stopped along the edge of the road. Their drivers were out walking over the area, looking at the skid marks and joking with one another.

"They ought to have that corner marked better. I've told them and told them . . ."

"Say, Tom, when's your boy getting back to the

78

States—pretty soon now, isn't it? Will he have to go back to Viet Nam after this leave?"

"Did you hear whether Obermeiers' daughter had her baby yet? Oh, she did? Another girl. That's a shame; they wanted a boy so bad this time."

"That's Silent Henry's car, isn't it? I didn't think he still had a license. They oughtn't to let him drive, no better than he can see. He'll kill himself for sure. Or somebody else."

Robert felt a proprietary kind of protectiveness for Henry. He went back to the police car and stood beside him, sheltering the old man from the onlookers. He started to pat Henry's shoulder, then didn't, for fear Henry might not want him to.

By now the car was on its wheels and had been hauled up onto the road. The tow-truck driver and one of the patrolmen were kneeling near the car, studying its undersides.

"I think she'll go okay," one of the men said. "Her wheels are all clear, and I can't see that anything's busted under there. Boy, that was lucky. I've seen new cars totaled out, with no worse a roll than this one had."

The patrolman approached, looking with concern at Henry, who was still visibly shaken.

Robert said, "Marv, how about if I drive Henry home? I've got my license now. And I'll stay with him till he feels better."

Marv looked relieved, Henry looked relieved, and the onlookers began to break up and drive away. Robert stopped one of them, the Shorts' next door neighbor, and asked her to tell his mother where he was, and that he would be late getting home.

The ride down the hill and out the mine road was a quiet one except for the car, which began making a rhythmic thudding sound halfway home. Robert drove slowly out of respect for the car's possible damage and for Henry's nervousness. But at length they coasted down across the tracks to the pink brick house.

Inside the house, Robert awkwardly took Henry's arm and steered him toward the davenport.

"You just lie down and relax for a while, and I'll make us some coffee. Or would you rather have a beer, or what?"

"Cup of coffee would be fine. Thank you, Robert. It was awful nice of you to bother about me."

Robert felt a glow of goodness. He grinned down at Henry, and for once he was not aware of the charm of his smile. For the time being he was not thinking at all about the siege. He filled the coffee-pot and got down two cups and saucers and sugar for his cup. During the past week of visiting Henry he had developed a tolerance for the bitter taste of coffee. He almost liked it.

"How does your shoulder feel by now?" He went to Henry and did a little gentle probing. Henry winced.

"Look in the bottom drawer of the bureau," Henry said. "There's a hot-water bottle in there. I believe a little heat'll draw some of the soreness out."

In the drawer, with the hot-water bottle and a pair of faded pajamas, was the man-shaped ginseng root. Robert paused long enough to take it out and study it for a moment by the light from the half-circle window. As it had the first time he saw it, the withered root-face seemed to take on features and expression as Robert stared at it. It felt warm to the touch, almost frighteningly lifelike. He put it back and went to fill the water bottle.

"I wonder if those ginseng men really do have any

power to bring good luck," he said, to take Henry's mind off the accident.

"Nah," Henry said. "The only good luck I ever expect out of that is the money I could get for it if I ever got hard up and had to sell it." But his mind was clearly still on the accident. As Robert laid the hot-water bottle on his shoulder, Henry said, "I don't reckon I should be driving anymore. I'm a menace on the highways. I tell you, Robert, I made that turn up there, and I'd of sworn I was right in the middle of the road. I wasn't, at all, I was clean off in the ditch before I hardly knew what hit me. I could have got killed."

Robert poured the coffee and brought the TV tray with the two cups on it over to where Henry could reach it. Then he sat down on the footstool.

"Henry, listen, this isn't any of my business, and you can tell me to butt out if you want, but I consider myself a friend of yours, and I can't help worrying a little about this whole thing. I mean, next week starts the ginseng season, right? And this is your whole source of income for all of next year, isn't it?"

Henry averted his eyes from Robert as he picked up his coffee and tested to see if it was cool enough to drink. It wasn't.

Robert went on. "Well, if you don't drive, or can't drive, how can you get to your ginseng beds? They're not close enough to walk to, are they?"

Henry snorted and shook his head.

"Then it seems to me that you've got a problem. Now, this is just a suggestion, but why don't you let me drive you? We could go in the afternoons after school and on weekends, or for that matter I could miss a few days of school, or even a couple of weeks. My folks wouldn't care a bit, and my mom's on the school board.

She could fix it up with the principal."

Henry was silent, expressionless.

"That would solve your problem, wouldn't it, Henry? I'd even help you dig. You'd get more ginseng than you could working alone. What's wrong with the idea? I'd be glad to do it. Really."

For a long moment Henry looked directly into Robert's eyes. Finally it was Robert who looked away.

Henry spoke slowly, almost belligerantly. "I go by myself or I don't go."

Exasperation mounted in Robert and tinged his voice. "Well, for Pete's sake, if you won't let me help you, will you at least go see if you can get some better glasses or something, so you won't be wrapping yourself around the first telephone pole you come to?"

Henry looked away.

"Look, tomorrow's Saturday. I know there's at least one optometrist over at Elkader who has office hours on Saturday. Will you at least let me drive you over there and see if he can do something for you?" His voice rose to a demanding level.

Henry looked up at him again, and this time the man's face was open and warm and unguarded.

"I expect that'd be all right," he said slowly. "If you want to bother."

"I want to bother."

The tension was broken. They talked about other things. Henry reminisced about how different schools were, back in his day. He asked about Robert's friends at school, and Robert shrugged off the question with a cryptic "I'm a loner."

When the room began to get dark, Robert cooked supper—a can of spaghetti and meatballs, a can of peas, bread and butter. They ate from the TV tray, laughing at how crowded it was.

While they ate and talked, Robert was thinking, I'm getting close. I'm really making headway now. But he's still not about to let me in on his ginsenging. That was dumb of me to offer to take him over to get his eyes looked at. If he couldn't drive, he might get desperate enough to let me drive him, and then I'd find out. But, heck, he gave me a flat no to that suggestion, and I can't very well just forget about him, let him go driving around half blind. Maybe after he thinks it over, he'll be so grateful to me that he'll change his mind. Probably not, though. I've never seen such a stubborn old bird. I'm beginning to think my siege system isn't going to be any match for his stubbornness.

After Robert had cleaned up the supper dishes, re-filled the hot-water bottle, and left, Henry tried to sleep. At first whenever he closed his eyes, he saw the terrifying ditch coming toward his car's windshield, the sky revolving, the steering wheel floating near his head.

But eventually his mind focused on a much more pleasant vision. He and Robert were driving along through a sun-filled autumn world, heading for the Wyalusing beds, or the Sny Magill beds, or some mythical ginseng bed chocked with huge red-berried plants. The two of them were seated together on the moist earth, talking together, digging together. Henry could feel the damp black earth resisting the push of his stubby fingers. He felt the dirt packing in under his nails; he felt the woody length of a giant ginseng root between his finger-tips as he followed it deeper and deeper into the ground, tracing its side shoots, getting every bit of it out. Between him and the boy there was no tension about whose ginseng it was, no secrets to guard. There was only friendship, the companionship of two human beings, never mind about ages or other differences. Just a friend to talk to.

With passion he hadn't felt since he had been Robert's age, he murmured, "Son, I wish I could take you with me. I wish I could."

11

When Robert knocked at Henry's door the next morning, to drive him to the optometrist's office, he was surprised to find Henry scrubbed and shaved and combed,
wearing an old but presentable blue suit. The red-and-
brown plaid shirt under the suit jacket dimmed the effect
somewhat, but even so, this morning Henry looked more
like someone's grandfather going to church than a gin-
seng-hunting river recluse.

"How's your shoulder this morning?" Robert asked
as they got into his father's car.

"Oh, not so bad, not so bad. It was awful stiff during
the night, though. Didn't hardly get any sleep at all,
and I got some bruises coming out. My face was so sore
I couldn't hardly shave it, over on this side here. My ribs
is a little sore, too. I must have hit them on the steering
wheel. But I guess I'll pull through."

They rolled along the mine road, past Robert's house,
past the boat dock and bait stand and hotel. Robert
touched the horn and lifted a hand to the two old men on
the hotel steps.

"Morning, Tom, Grampa Severs."

They turned and began the long winding ascent between the narrow row of houses that made up Buck
Creek's main street. Amber Showalter was standing on

the footbridge in front of her house, wearing tight-legged jeans and a sweat shirt. She was hanging small rag rugs over the peeled-sapling handrail of the little bridge. Robert touched the horn and waved. She turned, blushed when she saw him as she usually did, and waved back. Robert had a sudden warm feeling that Amber was happier for having seen him. He wondered, fleetingly, whether he might be overlooking a good thing in Amber. At least somebody to talk to, maybe, even if he didn't much feel like taking her out.

"Was that your girl, back there?" Henry asked suddenly.

"Not really. We're in the same class, is all." He might have said more, but he had detected a note in Henry's question that warned him not to, a note of wariness, of slightly forced lightness. It was almost as though Henry would have felt just a bit betrayed to learn that Robert had another friend beside himself.

A part of Robert's mind explored and digested this possibility, the possibility that Henry was becoming genuinely dependent on Robert's friendship.

They were coming up out of the valley now, emerging from between the walls of layered stone and clinging trees, up into the sunshine of the high level land. The fifteen-mile stretch from here to the county seat was newly paved and lightly traveled highway, curving around substantial farmsteads that had been there long before the highway, and remained staunchly in place while the highway made its respectful detour around them.

The open, empty road and the power of his father's car tempted Robert, but he held back, for fear Henry might be a little nervous about riding at high speeds after his accident.

Robert said, "We were lucky to get you an appointment at such short notice. Have you ever been to Dr. Hulich before?"

"Nah, I ain't been to an eye doctor since we lived—since I was working at the button factory that time. Must have been twenty-five years or more."

Robert was silent for a while. He tried to find some good music on the radio, but failed. "I sure hope you won't have to wait very long to get your new lenses, if he prescribes them, and I'm sure he will if it's been twenty-five years since you got your eyes checked. I think it usually takes about a week for them to order new lenses. That's what my mom's took, anyway."

Henry made a noncommittal answering sound.

"You'd probably get them by the end of the week. They'll mail them to you, if you don't want to come over and get them. Or if you do, I'll be glad to run you over here again next Saturday. I don't mind a bit."

"We'll see," Henry said.

"When had you planned to start digging your ginseng?"

"Planned to start this next week. Monday."

"That soon? I thought it was usually the second week in October that you started." Robert's mind was running on ahead.

"Nope," Henry said.

"Well, listen now, Henry, don't take this the wrong way or anything, but I don't see why you won't let me drive you. There's nothing I'd rather do than spend a few days out in the woods, just you and me, digging ginseng. I know my folks would let me take off from school. And I'd promise not to tell anybody where the beds are, if that's what you're worried about."

Henry's answer came back fast and sharp, and so

unexpected that the car swerved minutely under the impact of it.

"Now, you listen here, Robert Short, I know you're trying to find my ginseng beds, and you've *been* trying, ever since you was knee-high to a low toad, and I know that's the only reason you been hanging around me all week. Well, I admit I been kind of enjoying the chance to talk to somebody besides my four walls. But not you nor anybody else is ever going to sweet-talk me into handing over my ginseng beds. Them beds is all that stands between me and the county home, and all they mean to you is a chance to outsmart a worthless old man and make a little easy money to throw away, when you don't really need it."

His words echoed through the car, blending with the singing of the tires and the soft roar of the wind against the metal body.

Robert felt exposed; defensive, almost ashamed, and exposed.

"You've got it all wrong, Henry," he said with all the sincerity at his command. "Oh, sure, I wouldn't mind a chance to dig a little ginseng this fall, but that wasn't it. I really enjoy being with you, talking to you and listening to you. I meant it when I told you I don't have any close friends, and, well, I was beginning to think of you as one. Everybody needs somebody they can, you know, confide in. If you thought I was just after your ginseng, well, I'm just sorry you don't have any more faith in me than that."

They rode in silence the rest of the way to the doctor's office. In the waiting room, Robert made a few comments under his breath about the decor and the other patients. Henry answered with monosyllables that were gruff at first, but became increasingly less gruff under the warming influence of Robert's determined good humor.

After a half-hour wait, Henry was called into the examining room and Robert could relax and study the revelation.

He's known all along what I was after, Robert thought. And he never said anything. He's been friendly. We've had all those long talks, and he showed me his ginseng man. He's treated me like a friend, and all the time he knew I was just trying to butter him up. Why didn't he boot me out, as soon as he figured what I was up to?

The clock on the opposite wall marked off the minutes with electronic precision while Robert strained to understand.

Is it because Henry is such a really good person that he forgave me? No, that doesn't make sense. Could the old boy be so hard up for companionship that he was willing to have me around, to have the fake kind of friendship I was offering him, rather than none at all?

The clock moved on, in tiny minute-sized spasms. Robert's growing instinct for understanding the motives of others, the instinct that was so valuable in manipulating teachers and parents, told him that this last idea was probably the truth, or close to the truth. The dawning of this understanding brought with it a weight, the bothersome but somehow warming burden of responsibility for Henry's feelings.

Robert shook his head slowly as his thoughts moved on. Boy, he must have really hurt when he realized I wasn't just hanging around because I liked him. That I was trying to get something out of him.

He was shaken by the knowledge that he, Robert Short, actually had the power to hurt another human being, not by any act of deliberate cruelty but simply by being the kind of person he was. It was an unpleasant realization.

He stared, unseeing, at the toes of his shoes while he explored the idea. Several months ago he had made a silent vow to be as honest with himself as he possibly could at all times. Fib to other people if necessary, but never to himself. That was the crux of his theory. Since that time he had made an effort, whenever he thought about it, to admit to himself the real reasons why he did things, or said things, as he did. Already the practice had proved a big help in understanding himself.

Now he put it to its most painful test, and thought about the people in his life whom he was probably hurting without realizing it any more than he had with Henry.

He saw Amber Showalter in her old jeans, beating rag rugs on the footbridge this morning. By a tremendous concentration of his will, he put himself in her position as she stood there, homely and Saturday-morning messy, while the one person in her world she longed to impress drove by and saw her. Robert felt a pang of compassion.

But his mind would not stay, for long, away from Henry. *Now that I think about it from his angle, the whole siege idea was kind of a dirty trick. I just never really thought how it might be, on Henry's end of the deal. But why didn't Mom and Dad stop me? They should have known, even if I was too stupid to. What good does it do to have parents, anyway, if they don't keep you from doing dumb, mean things like that. Why . . .*

Henry emerged from the inner office.

"All set?" Robert sprang to his feet and opened the door for Henry. When they were in the car, he said, "What did the doctor say?" A feeling of protectiveness, contrition, poured out of Robert toward the old man besides him.

"Got to have stronger lenses," Henry said. He seemed

to have forgotten his earlier outburst. "Said my eyes was pretty good, though, for a fellow my age. I told him that came from living outdoors so much. I told him, 'Why, Doc,' I says, 'I've slept out on the ground more nights than you've slept in a bed.' I got to go back next Saturday and pick up the new specs. I told him you'd drive me over."

"Glad to." Robert grinned with relief that the tension was past.

After a few minutes of silent enjoyment of the autumn countryside, Henry said, "I expect you're saving up your money to buy an automobile. Time a boy gets his driver's license, it seems like he's got to have his own automobile these days."

"No, I'm not in any special hurry for that."

He started to answer Henry in the same way he had answered his parents and a few of the boys at school, when that question was brought up. But something stopped him, some urge toward stark honesty that grew out of his new understanding of how things stood between him and Henry. He told Henry what he had hardly had the courage to tell himself before.

"I'd like to have a car of my own. Who wouldn't? But the fact is I don't know a darned thing about what goes on under that hood up there. To me, it's just a confusing bunch of gears and stuff. I suppose I could learn, but mechanical things have never interested me. So, the thing is, if I bought an old car, which is all I could afford, all the guys at school would expect me to tear it down and fix it up, like they all do with theirs. The truth is, I've kind of tried to build up a reputation for myself as a pretty sharp guy, up here"—he tapped his temple—"and I'm afraid to spoil the image."

Henry said nothing.

Robert cleared his throat. "I guess that makes me seem like pretty much of a jackass, doesn't it?"

Suddenly, surprisingly, Henry's hand patted Robert's knee twice, then awkwardly withdrew.

Henry said, as he looked away from Robert out the window, "Ain't nobody in this world that's as good as he'd like people to think he is."

12

By the time Robert had dropped Henry off at the pink brick house and driven back home, it was after one. His house was empty. A note on the kitchen table told him that Mim had gone to Prairie du Chien and that there was plenty of Jell-O and sandwich ingredients in the refrigerator.

He carried his sandwich from room to room, pausing in front of one window after another, eating a bite or two and staring out at the river, the side yard, the bluffs that crowded down close behind the house. His mind was too charged with the Henry situation to allow him to sit down.

Somewhere in the confusion of emotions, he thought, the whole idea of the siege had gotten covered over. He still wanted the ginseng crop; he still wanted the money. But things were beginning to slip out of his control. Robert no longer clearly understood what it was that he did want from Henry.

He tried to imagine what his feelings would be if Henry were to come through that door, right now, and offer to show Robert the way to the ginseng beds.

I'd be disappointed in him, that's what, he thought. The realization surprised and amused him. I'd take him up on it, and I'd dig ginseng till my arms fell off, but yet

I'd sort of hate the thought of that stubborn old guy giving in to me.

He shook his head at the complexity of man, and finished his sandwich. He thought about Jell-O, but decided not to bother. His Saturday chinchilla chores still waited.

Downstairs, he snapped on the light in the chinchilla room and began gathering the glass-tubed water bottles for their weekly scalding.

"I bet you thought I'd forgotten you this morning, didn't you?"

His answer was the metallic rustling of claws on wire cage floors, as twenty-one smoke-and-white fur balls hopped to the fronts of their cages to watch for possible raisin treats. They sat up on their small but powerful hind legs, white bellies exposed, thick brush tails curling up behind, whiskers twitching.

It wasn't until he began replacing the water bottles in the bottom tier of cages that Robert saw what he had been hoping with all his might not to see. The two four-month-old babies in the middle cage, the fist-sized youngsters fathered by Ace, were no longer smooth and plump and beautiful. Their plushy blue-gray fur ended in ragged lines, halfway back from head to tail. The back half of each animal showed only a charcoal stubble, with occasional wisps of longer fur that their teeth had missed. They looked grotesquely deformed, all the more so because of the bright-eyed innocence in their tiny faces.

Robert sank to the floor and sat, head pressed against his knees, trying not to see what he had just seen.

"Oh, no," he said, over and over. "Oh, no. I was so sure it wasn't going to happen. Ace, how could you do this to me? And you two, *why* did you have to be chewers?"

He pulled the weight of his gloom down hard around

him. The concrete floor was uncomfortable, and he welcomed the discomfort. It was something to grind into, so he wouldn't have to think about Ace.

Ace. Beautiful, valuable Ace, who could have been such a triumph—given to him free by a veteran breeder, cured of his chewing by Robert's care, and subsequently sold for a clear profit of hundreds of dollars. Ace, still beautiful to look at but worthless to Robert or to any other breeder.

After a while, when it began to seem silly to go on sitting on the basement floor with his head on his knees, Robert got up and finished his work. On feet weighted with disappointment, he trudged upstairs and into the living room, where his father was just settling in for an afternoon of beer and football.

Don looked up at his son. "I wondered if you were around here somewhere. I couldn't find anybody when I came in. What makes you such a ball of sunshine this afternoon? You didn't have an accident with the car?"

"No, I didn't have an accident. I've got a problem though, Dad. Are you watching this?"

"Not yet. It's just the pregame interviews and stuff. Turn it off. What's your problem—did some of your stocks decline on Wall Street today?"

Robert gave him a withering look. "Are you going to be serious about this, or are you going to do a vaudeville routine while my whole chinchilla investment goes out the window?"

Don was immediately serious "What's wrong with the chinchillas?"

"Fur-chewing," Robert said darkly, as he sank into a corner of the davenport. He sat horizontally, his body sprawling into the room, his chin against his chest. His fingers picked at the frayed edge of his jeans as he laid one dangling foot across the other knee. A scrap of newspaper clung to the sole of his shoe; he plucked it off before his mother could accuse him of tracking chinchilla dirt through her house.

His father waited for the rest of the story. Robert went on. "Those two oldest babies of Ace's, those two real promising little females, you know? Well, they started chewing." He sighed. "You should see them, Dad. They look horrible."

"Let me get this straight, now. Ace is the one Mr. What's-his-name threw in free, because he was a fur-chewer, right?"

"Right. But then after I got him home he stopped chewing, so I thought it would be okay to use him for breeding, because he had better fur quality than my other males. And I thought if he didn't pass on the fur-chewing trait, I could turn around and sell him this winter at one of the chinchilla shows. I know he's good enough to be in the ribbons if I showed him, and that would make him worth a good three-hundred dollars, selling him to another breeder.

"But now"—Robert struck his knee—"I don't know what to do with him. I suppose what I really should do is wait till he's in prime, kill him and pelt him, and at least get twenty-five or thirty bucks for the pelt. But I hate like the devil to pass up that big money."

He waited, but his father said nothing, so he went on. "Of course, I *could* go ahead and show him and sell him, like I planned. I wouldn't *have* to say anything about the chewing."

Still Mr. Short said nothing. He just looked thoughtful.

Robert continued. "It probably wouldn't be very honest, selling him that way. But if the buyer didn't come right out and ask me if Ace was a chewer, there wouldn't be any outright lie involved. Would there?" He was beginning to feel impatient at his father's silence.

"Well, Dad? What do you think I should do?"

"I'm afraid I don't know enough about the chinchilla business to tell you what to do. They were your idea, and so far you've been doing a good job with them. A good, businesslike job. Your mother and I have been proud of you."

"Yes, but, Dad, you're not answering my question."

Mr. Short glanced at the dead television screen. "Now, Robert, I'm not going to tell you how to run your chinchilla business. You don't try to tell me how to run my silica mine." He smiled. "All I can say is, it's a 'caveat emptor' world. That means 'Let the buyer beware.' You'll find out, when you go to buy a used car or a house; nobody who has something to sell is going to point out its flaws to you. If you aren't sharp enough to find out for yourself what shape that car is in, or that house or whatever, then you deserve to get stuck. It seems to me it must be the same in the chinchilla business. I'd certainly think twice about passing up three-hundred dollars, if I were you."

Robert got up and started out of the room. He came back, turned on the television set, then left. His father seemed not to notice that he was gone.

He went outside to balance on the rim of the front porch. The sky was clouded over now. The wind that came off of the river had a feel of winter in it.

Ordinarily the river held little interest for Robert, but this afternoon the pewter dullness of the water suited his mood. He crossed the road, descended the embankment, and stepped from one rail to the other crossing the tracks. An obviously home-made flight of steps led down to an equally jerry-built dock, where his father's fiber

97

glass runabout bobbed and tugged gently at its tether.

With little thought about destination Robert jerked the motor into life and headed downriver, going as slowly as possible and staying near the shore, away from the treacherous main-channel current. He didn't want to have to pay attention to what he was doing. After a few minutes, when home was out of sight, he cut the motor and drifted.

Okay, Short, he argued silently, what's the matter with you now? Dad told you just exactly what you wanted to hear. You have his parental blessing to unload Ace for as much as you can get out of him. What did you expect out of dear old Dad, anyway, the Golden Rule?

He felt restless, letdown somehow. When Henry's house came into sight, through the riverbank trees, Robert found himself beaching the boat where Henry's back lawn became sandy shoreline.

Henry answered Robert's knock with the semidazed expression of one just awakened from a nap. His shoes were off. The davenport behind him held a crumpled afghan and the hot-water bottle.

"I'm sorry to bother you again so soon," Robert said as he came in and sat down in the big chair. "Why don't you lie back down, Henry? We can talk as well that way. Is your shoulder still hurting?"

"Litte bit," Henry grunted. He stretched out and rearranged the afghan and water bottle. "Old bones mend slow, boy. You get stiff muscles, and the stiffness don't go away like it does when you're young."

"Oh, you're not old," Robert scoffed. He could think of nothing else to say. He sat quietly for a few moments, hands clasped between his knees, watching Henry. The man's face looked oddly thinner, younger. Robert finally decided it was because Henry was lying on his back, so that the excess flesh of cheeks and jowls sank away un-noticed. It reminded Robert of the way his Uncle Alvord had looked, lying in his coffin at the funeral several years ago. It had been unmistakably Uncle Alvord, and yet a more youthful, more brightly colored, smoother Uncle Alvord than Robert had remembered.

The silence was becoming awkward. Partly because it was so much on his mind, and partly because he was sud-denly curious about Henry's reaction, Robert began to tell him about Ace, the fur-chewing babies, the problem he was faced with.

"If you were me, Henry, what would you do?"

Henry rolled his head toward Robert and opened one eye. "You asking me for advice, are you?"

Robert shrugged. "I guess so. I talked to my dad about it, and he seemed to think I'd be a sucker not to unload Ace for the three-hundred dollars."

"What's your problem then?"

Again Robert shrugged. "I don't know—it just doesn't seem to me like that would be the right thing to do. I know the really *right* thing would be to pelt Ace out, get rid of all his babies, and mark the whole thing up to experience."

"Then why don't you?"

"Is that what you think I should do, Henry? You've been around a lot, and I value your opinion. If you were in my place, is that what you'd do?"

Henry sat up and handed the water bottle to Robert. "This damn thing is cold again, pardon my French. You want to warm it up for me? Put on the coffeepot while you're up, why don't you," he added as Robert started for the kitchen.

"One thing about it," Robert called. "If I knowingly sold a fur-chewer at breeding-stock prices, it would probably give me a bad reputation later on, when I'll have other animals to sell. It might be worth it in the long run to take a loss on Ace."

"Honesty is the best policy," Henry called back.

Robert muttered wryly, "Gee, I wish I'd said that."

"What's that you said?"

"Nothing, Henry." He screwed the stopper into place and dried off the red rubber body of the bag. "Here you go, nice and hot."

He gave the bottle to Henry, then went back to the kitchen to start the coffee. As he brought down the cups and saucers, he thought, You know, I'm beginning to think there's more to this old boy than people realize. He might not have much in the way of education, and he's not the world's greatest conversationalist by a long shot, but down underneath it all, there's a kind of strength he's got. He's poor, and yet he's his own man. He doesn't owe anybody a thing. He's independent and he's—strong. Robert snorted silently. I'm really beginning to like the old grizzly.

Robert set the steaming cups on the TV tray between them.

"Henry, I just decided. You are one-hundred percent right. I'll pelt out Ace, and I won't use any of his babies for breeding. That's really a load off my mind. After this, you get first crack at solving all my problems, okay? Now about girls . . ."

They laughed together.

_____ **13** _____

Through the creeping hours of the night Henry lay
watching the reflection of the river on his ceiling. It wasn't
the ache of his muscles that kept him awake; it was the
soreness of enforced honesty.

You old fake, he said to himself. That's all you are,
Henry Leffert, a worthless old liar. 'Honesty is the best
policy.' Makes me want to heave my supper.

He closed his eyes and saw the bright face, the alarm-
ingly, painfully dear face of Robert smiling down at him,
handing him his water bottle. Henry turned his head
toward the wall.

That boy thinks I'm—good. How long has it been since
anybody had that kind of faith in me? Ruth used to, when
we was young. God, it scares me.

He tossed against the restricting tangle of the blankets about him. The hot-water bottle dropped to the
floor with an unnoticed slosh.

What if he was to find out what kind of a man Henry
Leffert really is? he fretted. What if he knew all I've done
in my time? Do you think he'd waste his time coming
around here? Not on your grandmother's shinbone he
wouldn't. What am I going to do?

The tangle of blankets around his arms and legs was
becoming unbearable. He kicked them off and sat up,

wincing, to look out the window. There was still no pink glow of sunrise beyond the Wisconsin bluffs. Sighing, he lay back down.

Why can't people just like each other, without . . . His mind dead-ended against the unadmittable fact, the core of his misery, the fact that he needed, desperately, the touch of love, and yet he could not stand the ties of it.

Gradually his thoughts stopped circling in their painful track and veered off along more constructive lines.

I been here too long, anyway. Twenty years in one town. That's not for Henry Leffert. Where, though? Back to Ruth, if she's still there? Maybe. Maybe not. More than likely she won't want me back, after all this time. Can't blame her. I wonder how it might be farther south, this time of year, Missouri or Arkansas? But I don't have any money, and it'd be a shame to leave before the ginseng harvest, when there's a whole year's worth of food-money waiting for me over to the Wyalusing beds.

Suddenly he threw off the blankets and stood up. The ache in his shoulders was gone, or at least overlooked, now. By the water-reflected moonlight that came in through the windows, he began moving around the room, opening bureau drawers, pulling things out of corners.

I'll do like I used to, camp up at the Wyalusing beds for a few days and dig till I've cleaned every particle of ginseng root out of that timber. Why, I've slept more nights out on the ground than . . .

Kneeling stiffly, he pulled from under the bed his old sleeping bag. His face was alight with the excitement of approaching adventure.

I'll stay up there a few days, till I've dug as much as that station wagon will carry. Then I'll start south. I'll find something along this old river. I found Buck Creek, didn't I, and this place here? Something else will turn up.

102

He stood and went to the window. A floating mansion, all four stories blazing with lights, came drifting down the river toward him. The *Casey*, he reckoned, on her way back down to St. Louis with a load of empties.

He watched until the *Casey* had passed the house and disappeared from sight. A kind of melancholy held him at the window.

No, I dasn't stay here, he told himself firmly. I'll go, and the boy won't ever know but what I really was the good kind of person he took me to be. And I won't have to worry anymore about the owners of this house showing up and finding me here. It's better all around if I go, and go now, before I spoil everything between the boy and me. Or before I get completely soft in the head and tell him where my ginseng is.

He got out his laundry carton and began putting into it the contents of the bureau drawers—his other pajamas, some shirts and underwear, a few pair of socks and long drawers, a couple of handkerchiefs.

Come to think of it, if I'm leaving here, I don't reckon it would do me any harm to tell Robert how to find the Sny Magill bed. I won't have time or car space to dig it and Wyalusing both.

He rocked back on his heels, frowning. No, by God, I ain't going to give in to him. If he wants them beds, he can just go out and hunt them like I had to. It ain't good for him to grow up thinking he can sweet-talk people like he tried to do me.

The sky beyond the Wisconsin bluffs was going from black to apple-green. Henry noticed it and went back to work. He pulled open the bottom drawer, then paused again. His mind was still filled with Robert, with the brightness and warmth the boy had brought into the pink brick house. Slowly, thoughtfully, Henry picked up the root man. For a long time he sat on his stiffening haunches and looked down at the withered root.

If I just sneak off without any kind of good-bye to the boy, and never come back here, he mused, why, in a week or so Robert won't even remember there was a Henry Leffert. Then if Ruth don't want me back, there really wouldn't be anybody to care if I was to die. And I could, too. These chest pains of mine could be a heart attack coming on, or I could have a bad car accident. And nobody would even come to the funeral.

He thought for another few minutes, weighing the alternatives; then he stood up. Under the bed he found an old shoebox full of fossil rocks. He tossed the rocks out the front door and carefully, lovingly, fit the ginseng man into the box.

The sun was clear of the bluffs now. Moving quickly, before he had time to regret his decision, Henry began carrying his belongings out to the car.

_____ **14** _____

As was usually the case on Sunday morning, Robert was awake long before his parents. In his pajamas and tennis shoes he descended to the kitchen and began to scramble a couple of eggs. He enjoyed making his own breakfast. He could have his eggs the way he liked them, moist and smooth, without that little tough crust his mother's eggs always had. As he started the fire under last night's left-over coffee, he smiled.

Here I am drinking coffee and liking it, he thought. Henry's influence.

It reminded him of a line from a poem his literature class had had to memorize last year. "Nor knowest thou what argument thy life to thy neighbor's creed has lent."

He had memorized it, but the words had merely skimmed the surface of his understanding. Their rhythm and antiquated phrasing had deflected his attention from what the words were saying. But now, months later, they came back up from the bottom of his mind where they had been digested and understood.

People affect each other without knowing it, without meaning to.

Robert cocked his head slightly. It was an interesting thought, a fascinating thought. He explored it further while his fork remained poised over his eggs.

Henry unknowingly got me started drinking coffee. That was just a little thing, though. Let's see now—that kid in swimming class got me into the chinchilla business just by dropping a casual remark. I wonder who else has affected my life. Parents, of course. They're probably the ones that started me thinking about earning all that money. Not that Dad ever said much about it, in words, but there's no doubt they've encouraged me.

On the other hand, there's the deal about Ace. It's Henry's advice I'm going to take on that, not Dad's. I wonder if Henry is affecting me in other ways.

His mind began to replay the scenes of the past week—the siege, which had started as a challenging game and had ended yesterday in exposure and a flush of shame; the words and emotions that he and Henry had exchanged . . . and withheld. For a long time he sat in silence. Finally a realization poured through him.

Yes. Henry has had an effect on me. After I got to know him, I didn't want his ginseng anymore. And I think I'm actually glad he didn't give in to me.

The thought carried subtle truths he didn't want to explore right now. He let it sink down in his mind to be understood weeks or months or maybe years from now.

He began to eat as his thoughts jumped to an even more interesting facet of the whole business of people affecting each other.

I wonder whose life *I* might have changed without knowing it. It was an exciting possibility.

Let's see now, parents don't count. I'd be bound to have made lots of changes in their lives. Who else? Amber?

Amber—whose long unlovely face was nearly as familiar to Robert as his own, and yet somehow unfamiliar. He hadn't really looked at it for a long time. Good old

106

Amber, who had years ago accepted the fact of his superiority, had stood up miserably but loyally under his little-boy cruelties, and now bore his smaller but more painful cruelties of nonrecognition.

I probably have affected Amber's life. They say a woman never completely gets over her first love, and maybe I've been Amber's first love and didn't even know it.

The possibility gave him an odd protective feeling toward Amber.

He went upstairs and dressed; then, moving quietly because he enjoyed the feel of being the head of the house while his parents slept, he went down into the basement. As he entered the chinchilla room, Ace hopped to the front of his cage to greet him.

"Sorry, boy," Robert said sadly, "but you're going to have to be somebody's fur coat before very long."

He looked away from the bright black eyes that watched him, and stooped to lift Big Mama from her cage. With her warm fur against his cheek, he walked to the basement window and looked out. Her whiskers tickled his nose, but the weight of her on his shoulder, depending on him not to drop her, was a welcome burden.

The window faced the river, and the road. As Robert stood there, still dreamy with his breakfast-table speculations, a car approached. The lawn's embankment and the fence blocked most of the car from his sight, but what he could see looked like Henry's old blue station wagon. Robert was surprised to see the car roll to a stop beside the Shorts' big rural mailbox. Faintly he heard the click–click of the mailbox being opened and shut; then the car drove away.

That's funny, Robert thought. What would Henry be

leaving in our mailbox? I hope he's not driving very far, with those eyes of his.

Into Big Mama's torn and sagging ear he murmured, "I wonder whether I've affected Henry in any way. No —I guess not. Anybody that old and set in his ways isn't going to be changed by anybody, much less a kid. Old Henry's so stubborn, I can't imagine anything having much effect on him."

He was quiet for a long time, hearing but not really hearing the metallic rustling of the animals in their cages behind him.

Finally he said, thoughtfully, "Still, I'm kind of glad to have Henry for a friend."

LYNN HALL was born in a suburb of Chicago and was raised in Des Moines, Iowa. She has always loved dogs and horses and has kept them around her whenever possible. As a child, she was limited to stray dogs, neighbors' horses, and the animals found in library books. But, as an adult, she has owned and shown several horses and has worked with dogs, both as a veterinarian's assistant and a handler on the dog show circuit. Several of her books are about dogs and horses.

For several years Ms. Hall has devoted herself full-time to writing books for young readers. She also works as coordinator and counselor for a local telephone counseling service offering help to troubled young people. Her leisure time is spent reading, playing the piano, or exploring the nearby hills and woodlands on horseback or foot, with a dog or two at her heels.

AVON ◆ CONTEMPORARY READING
FOR YOUNG PEOPLE

☐	Fox Running R. R. Knudson	31914	$1.25
☐	The Cay Theodore Taylor	21048	$1.25
☐	The Owl's Song Janet Campbell Hale	28738	$1.25
☐	The House of Stairs William Sleator	32888	$1.25
☐	Listen for the Fig Tree Sharon Bell Mathis	24935	$ .95
☐	Me and Jim Luke Robbie Branscum	24588	$ .95
☐	None of the Above Rosemary Wells	26526	$1.25
☐	Representing Superdoll Richard Peck	25115	$ .95
☐	Some Things Fierce and Fatal Joan Kahn, ed.	32771	$1.50
☐	The Sound of Chariots Mollie Hunter	26658	$1.25
☐	Guests in the Promised Land Kristin Hunter	27300	$ .95
☐	Taking Sides Norma Klein	27599	$ .95
☐	Sunshine Norma Klein	33936	$1.75
☐	Why Me? The Story of Jennie Patricia Dizenzo	28134	$1.25
☐	Forgotten Beasts of Eld Patricia McKillip	25502	$1.50

Where better paperbacks are sold or directly from the publisher.
Include 25¢ per copy for postage and handling; allow 4-6 weeks for
delivery.

Avon Books, Mail Order Dept.
250 West 55th Street, New York, N.Y. 10019

CRY 5-77

Watership Down

A novel by
Richard Adams

"QUITE MARVELOUS . . . A POWERFUL NEW
VISION OF THE GREAT CHAIN OF BEING."
The New York Times

"A GREAT NOVEL . . . A CLASSIC . . .
DO NOT MISS THIS BOOK."
Los Angeles Times

"AN ADVENTURE STORY OF AN EPIC SCOPE . . .
I CANNOT IMAGINE THAT ANY SENSIBLE
READER COULD COME AWAY FROM THIS
NOVEL UNAFFECTED AND UNCHANGED."
Newsweek

 19810 $2.25

WATER 5-77

AVON ⬡ CONTEMPORARY READING
FOR YOUNG PEOPLE

~~~~~~

- [ ] **Pictures That Storm Inside My Head**
  Richard Peck, ed.   30080 $1.25

- [ ] **Don't Look and It Won't Hurt**
  Richard Peck   30668 $1.25

- [ ] **Dreamland Lake**   Richard Peck   30635 $1.25

- [ ] **Through a Brief Darkness**
  Richard Peck   21147 $ .95

- [ ] **Go Ask Alice**   33944 $1.50

- [ ] **A Hero Ain't Nothin' but a Sandwich**
  Alice Childress   33423 $1.50

- [ ] **It's Not What You Expect**   Norma Klein   32052 $1.25

- [ ] **Mom, the Wolfman and Me**
  Norma Klein   34405 $1.25

- [ ] **Johnny May**   Robbie Branscum   28951 $1.25

- [ ] **Blackbriar**   William Sleator   22426 $ .95

- [ ] **Run**   William Sleator   32060 $1.25

- [ ] **Soul Brothers and Sister Lou**
  Kristin Hunter   28175 $1.25

- [ ] **A Teacup Full of Roses**
  Sharon Bell Mathis   20735 $ .95

- [ ] **An American Girl**   Patricia Dizenzo   31302 $1.25

~~~~~~